I0456800

The Bloody Note Murder

A Jake Malloy Mystery

Frank Kozusko

This is a work of fiction. Names, characters, places, and incidents are products of the author's imagination or are used fictitiously and are not to be construed as real. Any resemblance to actual events, locations, organizations, or persons, living or dead, is entirely coincidental.

World Castle Publishing, LLC
Pensacola, Florida
Copyright © Frank Kozusko 2021
Paperback ISBN: 9781956788006
eBook ISBN: 9781956788013
First Edition World Castle Publishing, LLC, October 18, 2021
http://www.worldcastlepublishing.com
Licensing Notes
Cover: Karen Fuller

Editor: Maxine Bringenberg

CHAPTER ONE

The smell of hamburger grease rose into my second-floor space. What else could I expect with a private eye office above a hamburger joint? But the rent was cheap, and Chuck, the owner, didn't give me any grief about sleeping in the office despite the zoning laws.

One thing did bother me: the flashing red light from Chuck's sign. The two-sided sign ran vertically up the building outside my office window. From dusk until the 10:00 p.m. closing, it would flash CHUCK'S, sending its red beams across my desk, alternating the shadows in my dimly lit office from a thin gray to a dilute pink.

Chuck's burgers were good. Sometimes in the mornings, I'd get breakfast when Chuck's wife, Meg, ran the place. They let me run a tab.

Chuck was a soft touch for veterans down on their luck. We were both ex-GIs five years back from the war, Chuck in the army in Europe and me in the coast guard in the Pacific.

Thursday afternoon signaled the coming end of the workweek for most civilians, but not for a struggling P.I. I would take any job I could get; nights, weekends, didn't matter. I finished the notes on my latest assignment; a typical case, tailing some gal, trying to get the goods on her. This one had a twist. A rich father, not a jealous husband, had hired me. He had forbidden his young daughter from keeping company with a guy the old man considered a fortune hunter. My report would be enough for the old man to disinherit her if that's what he wanted to do. I had plenty of incriminating photos being developed at the drugstore down the street. My plan was to get the prints first thing in the morning and hand-deliver the package. I was hoping the old man would pay me COD.

So, with the day's tasks completed on my sole case, I figured one of Chuck's burgers and a movie was in order for the rest of the evening.

Chuck was flipping burgers when I swung open his storefront door centered between the two plate-glass windows. His diner occupied a long, narrow rectangular space. The six booths against the wall on the left, and the thirteen stools at the counter on the right, featured bright red artificial leather-covered cushions and chrome trim. Behind the counter was the grill and the door and windows to the small kitchen and scullery. The linoleum floor featured black and white squares laid out in a diamond shape. There was a jukebox against the wall at the far end.

A small bell attached to the door announced my entrance. Chuck gave me a glance over his right shoulder. He was wearing his typical all-white counterman's garb: pants, T-shirt, and a little round brimless hat. His full around-the-neck apron had numerous grease stains. Not a big man, standing only about five-nine, he had retained his lean muscular U.S. Army physique that had carried him through D-Day and the Battle of the Bulge. Like most vets, Chuck didn't like to talk much about his wartime experiences. What little I knew of his time in service I had learned at our first meeting when I answered his newspaper ad for an office for rent. We had traded just enough info to cement our status as fellow veterans. He was a born and bred San Francisco boy, unlike many vets here, including myself, who fell in love with the city on our way through to the war and came back.

"Hey, Jake, how's it going?"

"Not bad, not bad," I replied, taking a seat at the empty counter. "How are you?"

"Okay, I guess. Let me finish up here, be right back." Chuck served up two cheeseburger and french fries platters, delivered them to a young couple in the far booth near the jukebox, then returned to his position behind the counter. "So, what'll it be?"

"Can I get a burger and some coffee on my tab? Should be getting a payday tomorrow, then I can settle up."

"Sure. Okay."

"Thanks, Chuck."

Chuck poured a coffee, then turned and

dropped a hamburger patty on the grill. He remained unusually quiet while the sound of sizzling grease mixed with the swing music from the jukebox. I nursed my cup until Chuck delivered my burger and pushed the ketchup and mustard bottles next to the plate. Without a word, he refilled my coffee.

"Chuck, is something wrong? You're kind of quiet tonight."

"Nah, just tired, I guess."

"Is Meg okay?"

"She's fine. Got her hair done today. That always makes her feel good."

Our conversation was interrupted when the girl from the last booth strode to the counter. "Can I get some quarters for the jukebox?" she asked, handing Chuck a one-dollar bill.

Without replying, he rang up NO SALE on the cash register, deposited the one, and retrieved four quarters. "Here you are," he said, handing her the change.

"You mind if we dance?" she asked.

Chuck smiled a little and shrugged his shoulders. "Yeah, all right. I don't have a license for that, but go ahead."

I nodded. "That's nice, Chuck."

"Aw, just letting the kids have some fun. Wasn't like that when we were their age."

"No. Not for us."

The swing music started up again. I finished my burger, then took the last slug of coffee. "I guess I'll take off now."

"What plans you got for the evening?" Chuck asked.

"I thought I'd catch a movie at the Bijou. This weekend they're showing movies made during the war. Tonight they got *Destination Tokyo*."

"Great submarine movie. Saw that one in England while waiting for the invasion." Chuck took a deep breath and exhaled forcefully. "I think I'll close up early as soon as they leave," he said, pointing with his head. "It's been slow; I let the dishwasher go home an hour ago."

"Well, so long," I said, spinning around on my stool. "See yah later."

"See yah."

As I left, the bobby-soxer girl and her

boyfriend were doing a mean jitterbug.

***

I was making my way back from the Bijou just before 9:00 p.m. when Chuck's place came into view. His flashing sign was off. *I guess Chuck did close early.*

But the inside lights were on, shining into the night. When I got close enough, my footsteps breaking the silence of the empty street, I could see the CLOSED sign hanging in the window. Guessing Chuck was still cleaning up, I went in to say goodnight. This time the jingling of the bell prompted no response. The place looked empty. "Hey, Chuck, you here?" I called, receiving no answer.

Spotting broken dishes scattered on the floor, I pulled out my gun, my pulse increasing. Holding my Colt .38 Special in the two-handed grip I had learned at P.I. school, I made my way to the open end of the counter, all the while shifting my gaze between the kitchen door and the doors to the restrooms.

Chuck was face down behind the counter; blood visible on the floor. I wanted to go to him, check if he was breathing or had a pulse, but my self-preservation instinct had me moving to the kitchen door. I swept that room and found it empty. Returning to Chuck without exposing my back to the restrooms, I checked his neck for a pulse. Not finding one, I turned him over. Chuck had been shot in the chest.

I finished securing the scene with a cautious search of the restrooms. My adrenaline quickly subsiding. I holstered my piece and made my way back to the counter. Only then did I note the open and empty cash drawer.

I had to step over Chuck's body to get to the phone to call the cops.

I turned on Chuck's sign and waited.

CHAPTER TWO

I had some time to think before the cops arrived. The empty cash drawer pointed to a robbery gone wrong. Robberies of small establishments like Chuck's are all for the quick bucks: flash a gun, grab the dough, and run. If this had been a robbery, something must have happened to change the dynamics. I looked at the broken dishes on the floor as a clue.

The revolver Chuck stored under the counter near the cash register was still in place. I envisioned Chuck coming from the kitchen with some clean dishes to be shelved and encountering an armed holdup attempt. Chuck was a veteran of hand-to-hand combat. He wasn't likely to be overly threatened by a brandished handgun. He'd thrown the stack of dishes at the robber in an attempted distraction, enough time for Chuck, he had hoped, to get his gun. If that's the way it went down, it hadn't worked. The robber had responded by shooting Chuck.

There was something else that gave a hint as to the timeline. The grill was stone cold but covered in grease. Chuck had turned off the grill but hadn't got to cleaning it before he was shot. I guessed it would take at least an hour for the grill to cool down. I found Chuck about nine, so the shooting must have occurred before eight. I had left for the movies at around six-thirty, leaving a window of an hour and a half.

***

I was still behind the counter when an armed patrol cop came through the door. "Freeze," he shouted. "Put your hands in the air and walk around to the front of the counter."

I sure didn't want to get shot by a nervous cop. I complied with all his commands. "I'm Jake Malloy. I found the body. I'm the one who called it in."

"Let's see some identification and make

it real slow."

Yeah, real slow. I reached into the breast pocket of my jacket and pulled out my wallet.

"Put it on the counter and step back," ordered the cop. He checked my ID. "Private eye, huh? You carrying?"

"Yes."

"Well, just as slowly, take it out and put it on the counter. Then go sit in the first booth. We'll wait for the detective."

It seemed like a long time waiting before the detective arrived, me cooling it in a booth and the cop, on a stool, pointing his gun. The patrol car with its flashing light had attracted the curious, who pressed against the windows to see what was happening. The detective had to push his way through the crowd to get to the door. I was happy to see Mike Farrell. We had worked a few cases together on a friendly basis.

"Jake, is that you? What have you gotten yourself into this time?" queried Farrell.

"Nothing I planned."

"I'll take it from here," Farrell informed the patrol cop. "Go take care of the crowd."

Farrell gave me back my gun. "What've you got?"

I showed Farrell Chuck's body. "Charles Darcy—Chuck, the owner." I pointed to the empty cash drawer. "Looks like a robbery."

"Yep, looks like a robbery. How do you happen to be here?"

I gave Farrell a rundown of events, how I had dinner at Chuck's, and left for a movie at six-thirty, back at nine, the dishes on the floor, Chuck's in-place revolver, and the cold grill. I shared my theory of the crime with him.

"Seems a plausible sequence," Farrell commented. "We've had a string of robberies of diners like this one in the last few weeks, but no shootings. Always the same M.O. A young couple comes in, they eat. They keep playing the jukebox as an excuse for hanging around until the place is empty. Then they pull a gun and demand the money from the register. The guys at the station are calling them the Jukebox Bonnie and Clyde."

I was stunned. Could that young couple I left Chuck with have been the Jukebox Bonnie and Clyde? The sequence and the timeline seemed right.

"Mike," I said sadly. "There was a young couple playing the jukebox and dancing when I left for the movies."

"Hmm. Can you describe them?"

"Both in their early twenties. The guy five-eleven, 180 pounds. He was wearing khaki pants and a blue button-up shirt. Short brown hair—not military, but short. Watch on his left wrist. The girl—brunette, five-three, 105 pounds, white blouse, red skirt, saddle shoes, and white bobby socks."

Farrell laughed, shaking his head. "That's some description. It's nice to have a gumshoe for an eyewitness. That matches the general description of Bonnie and Clyde. Anything else?"

"Yeah, I almost forgot. The girl had blue eyes. Nice perfume."

"Nice perfume! Really, Jake?"

"Well, she stood right next to me at the counter when she asked Chuck for change for the jukebox."

"Okay. I suppose you could pick them out of a lineup."

"No problem."

The patrol cop stuck his head through the doorway, interrupting our conversation. "Detective Farrell. Just got a report on the car radio. The coroner will be here in five minutes."

Farrell acknowledged, then turned back to me. "Jake, that's all I need from you right now. You can stay for the coroner if you want."

The big red Coca-Cola bottle top clock on the wall read 9:52. I thought about Meg waiting for Chuck to come home. "Thanks, Mike. I think I should inform Chuck's wife that she's a widow now. We're kind of friends. May be better to hear it from me. That okay with you?"

"Sure, Jake. Tell her I will be by in the morning, around ten, with some questions. What's her name and address?"

"Meg Darcy—I think her full name is Margaret. They have a place at 1437A Ortega Street."

"That's just a few blocks from here."

"Yeah, I'm going to walk over there

now."

"You still in that place on Lathrop Avenue?"

"Nope, I'm right upstairs. Chuck was my landlord. Here's my card."

"Okay. Goodnight, Jake."

"Goodnight, Mike."

The coroner's ambulance arrived, and the cops cleared a path through the crowd. I stepped aside as they rolled the gurney inside to retrieve Chuck's body.

I turned my collar up against the chill of the San Francisco evening and made my way to Meg.

CHAPTER THREE

The ten minutes it would take to walk from the diner to the modest house Meg and Chuck had bought when they married a year after the end of the war wasn't enough time for me to get my mind ready to see her. And I needed a drink. I decided to stop at Kelly's Irish pub along the way. She wouldn't be expecting Chuck home until his usual return time, around ten-forty-five. A quick stop would be okay as long as I talked to her before she started worrying about him being late.

Entering Kelly's, immersed in the displays of shamrocks, shillelaghs, the Irish flag, and some Irish brogues, I could imagine myself whisked to Dublin. Not everyone that frequented Kelly's was Irish; most seemed to be. Many were first-generation Irish Americans like the owner and bartender Sean (Johnny) Kelly; me, James Malloy; and Chuck, Charles Darcy. Chuck had introduced me to Kelly's shortly after I moved into the office. Many times we'd have a few beers together after Chuck closed the diner.

Kelly, who talked with a slight lilt, greeted me with surprise in his voice. "Jake, here by yourself tonight?"

I didn't reply. "Johnny, give me a shot of Jameson."

"Whiskey instead of beer! You must have something on your mind."

I threw the whiskey down my throat and asked for another one.

"Chuck coming by tonight?" Johnny asked as he filled my shot glass.

"Chuck ain't coming. He's dead. Shot in a holdup."

Johnny's face went pale. He grabbed the edge of the well-worn mahogany counter.

"Johnny, are you okay? You'd better sit."

He pulled over a stool he kept behind

the bar and sat down. His eyes filled. His hand shook as he reached for another shot glass, put it alongside mine, and poured. In a shaky voice, he asked, "What happened?"

"I found his body about nine. He'd been shot in the chest, cash drawer empty. The cops were still there when I left. I'm on my way to tell Meg."

Johnny made the sign of the cross on his body and looked up. "Jesus, take his soul. Poor Meg. I was best man at their wedding."

"I didn't know that."

"Yeah, me and Chuck go way back. We grew up in this neighborhood. When we graduated high school, we both got jobs working one or two days a week on the docks. Later, Chuck was a chauffeur. I applied for that job first, but I guess I sounded too Irish for a fancy limo service. I told Chuck about the job, and he got hired. Then the war came, and we both entered the service. Ain't that something? He survived the war and being wounded and gets killed for a couple of bucks."

"Yeah, that something all right—

something sad."

Johnny held up his glass. "To Chuck."

"To Chuck," I replied. We clinked our glasses and downed the whiskey.

"Hey, you're a P.I. You gonna investigate?"

"I'll do what I can. Right now, I have to see Meg."

"Okay. Tell Meg I'll give Chuck an old-fashioned Irish wake after the services right here in my bar."

"I'll tell her."

***

The Darcy's stucco bungalow, built in 1940, was one of the newer houses in the Sunset District. I had been a guest a few times for Sunday dinner. Chuck and Meg were both Catholic and preferred not to work on the Lord's day. The two-story building had a garage on the ground floor, an outdoor stairway leading to the porch, and their flat on the second floor. The lights awaiting Chuck's return home illuminated the steps.

Meg answered the door shortly after I

knocked. "Hi, Jake, What a pleasant surprise. Chuck's not home yet; should be soon. Come in."

"Thanks."

Meg was a diminutive woman who kept her brown hair short. At age twenty-nine, she was a few years younger than Chuck and me. She ushered me into the living room, turned off the radio, and offered me one of the stuffed chairs. "Sit here. Can I get you something, a beer?"

"No, thanks. I just came from Kelly's."

Meg sat on the sofa across from me. "Kelly's? You should have called Chuck and had him meet you there. He likes Kelly's, and I don't mind if he stops after work as long as he calls to let me know he'll be home late."

The time had come. I had to say something. "Meg, that's why I'm here. There was a robbery at the diner. Chuck was shot."

Meg starred at me for a second or two. "He's okay, right?"

I shook my head. "Sorry, Meg, Chuck's dead. I'm the one who found him. The cash drawer was empty; that's why I suspect a robbery."

Meg gasped, broke into heartrending sobs, and rushed to the bathroom. I could hear her vomiting. After a few minutes, she returned, bleary-eyed. She struggled to get the words out, asking, "When did it happen?"

"I think sometime between 6:30 and 8:00. I found him at nine in the diner and called the cops."

She got up. "I have to go. I have to see him."

I stood and put my hand on her shoulder. "The cops probably took Chuck to the morgue already. Maybe you can see him tomorrow."

Meg fell back onto the sofa and started to weep. I sat next to her, held her hand, and put my arm around her. She leaned into my chest and continued to cry. After a while, she straightened up. "I'll have to phone his brother. Liam is his only relative. Chuck's parents are dead."

Meg seemed to be recovering from the initial shock. I had to ask some questions. "It looks like a robbery, but we can't be sure. Was Chuck having any problems with anyone?"

"No. Everyone liked Chuck."

"Did he seem worried or nervous recently?"

"No. Everything was fine."

"Okay. Good. Is there anything I can do for you tonight? Maybe you want to call a friend to come over. I can wait."

"No. I'll be all right. Just stay with me a little longer."

I guessed she wasn't ready to be alone. "Of course. How about that beer?"

"Okay. I think I'll have one too. Can you get them? You know where I keep the glasses."

"Sure."

I knew my way around Meg's neat and tidy kitchen, having helped clean up after many of those Sunday dinners. I grabbed two beers from the refrigerator, filled two glasses, and returned to the parlor. Without saying a word, I handed Meg a glass. She took a small sip and placed her glass on the coffee table. I sat, sipping and holding my glass.

We talked for a while. Mostly, I let her do the talking. She related how she was a "Donut Girl" at the USO during the war. She met Chuck when he came home on leave before being shipped to Europe.

"We got married after he was discharged and lived in a small apartment for a few years. We bought this house on the GI Bill soon after I got pregnant." She paused. "But I had a miscarriage."

"I didn't know that. I am sorry."

"We were still trying, but now that will never happen. Oh, look at the time. I need to call Liam."

"Are you sure you don't want to call a friend?"

"No, I'll be okay. I think I want to be alone for a while. I'll call my mother. She'll probably come down from Grass Valley tomorrow."

"All right. Mike Farrell is the detective working the case. I know him; he's a good cop. He'll be coming to talk with you tomorrow morning, around ten. You won't be able to get into the diner; it'll be sealed as a crime scene.

You can ask Farrell when you can see Chuck.
I'll check in with you tomorrow too."

"Thanks, Jake."

"Oh, and Johnny Kelly wants to give
Chuck an Irish wake at his bar." I made my
way to the door. "Chuck was a great guy."

Meg just nodded. I could hear her sobbing
again as I closed the door.

When I reached the bottom of the stairs,
she turned off the outdoor lights.

Chapter Four

The alarm clock wrenched me from a deep sleep on Friday morning, too short a sleep that came in the shadowy hours before sunrise. I didn't typically set an alarm, but after Thursday evening's emotional events, I had a poor chance at much shuteye. And I had a schedule to keep, getting photos and making a report to a suspicious father. I got the coffee percolator going and hit the office bathroom for a quick washup and shave.

While I waited for the percolating liquid to bubble to a dark brown, I made toast and scrambled some eggs on my hotplate. Cooking in the office was another violation that Chuck had overlooked. I was listening to the radio news when Chuck's murder was reported:

"Charles Darcy, owner of Chuck's on 13th Avenue, was murdered last night in his diner during an apparent robbery. Police believe the crime to be linked to the Jukebox Bonnie and Clyde robbers, who are credited with a string of diner holdups. Darcy is the first victim to be shot and killed."

After breakfast, I packed a small bag with a clean shirt, socks, skivvies, and an undershirt. Meeting my client in his home called for a bit more cleanliness than my office bird bath afforded. My plan was to get a shower at the YMCA and change into my clean clothes, then pick up the photos from Murray's drugstore on the way back.

I hit the street, anticipating the grim scene awaiting me. Instead of Chuck's diner being filled with Meg's usual breakfast trade, the place was locked up and secured with police cords. I took a glance through the door glass; last night's broken dishes were still there on the floor. I turned away and headed for the Y.

A shower at the Y was always invigorating, and I really needed it that morning. I lingered in the stream of hot water washing over my head and body for quite some time, getting more than my money's worth from my membership dues, clean towels included. A renewed man, I arrived at the drugstore just as the photo service made the morning delivery. I got my prints, two sets, and made my way back to the office.

I carefully placed the photos in a chronology, using the negatives to check the ordering. Comparing the timeline to my notes, I wrote the date, time, and location on the back of each. I selected the ones that best told the story of the forbidden meetings between the daughter and her boyfriend, numbered them, and put them in an envelope with my written report. I kept the second set, likewise numbered and IDed, for my records.

***

My old Studebaker coupe, in dire need of a tune-up, struggled, as usual, on the Frisco slopes and up the crest to where my client, Carl Young, lived in the Potrero Hill neighborhood. Young was a retired businessman who had made a fortune in real estate, having had the foresight during the Great Depression to buy up acres of sand dunes, which were developed after the war to become the Sunset District.

I found a space to park not far from Young's Victorian mansion and grabbed my attaché case. A butler answered the doorbell ring.

"I'm Jake Malloy. I have an appointment to see Mr. Young."

"Mr. Young is expecting you. Please follow me," he said, then led me through the house to a large patio in the rear.

Young was seated, his back to me, at a table covered with a variety of breakfast items, a bowl of fruit, a coffee carafe, and several covered serving dishes.

"Good morning, Mr. Malloy. Please sit down."

"Good morning, sir," I replied, taking the chair he had indicated.

That was the second time I had visited the house; the first time was when Young hired me. Both times he'd remained seated, never standing to greet me. From our discussions, I had guessed his age at fifty. He and his wife had divorced when their only child, Lisa, was two years old. When Lisa was sixteen, her mother died, and Lisa came to live with Young. Their relationship had always been strained because of their geographical separation. Young had expressed his opinion that his ex-wife had poisoned Lisa against him. When she reached legal age, Lisa, though still financially dependent on her father, threatened to move out. Young saw the nineteen-year-old Lisa's relationship with a forty-five-year-old man, Bill Hunter, as her attempt to make good on the threat. Young viewed Hunter as living up to his name — a fortune hunter interested in getting at Young's money, somehow.

"Would you like some breakfast?" he asked.

"Thanks, maybe just some coffee."

Young nodded at the butler, who produced a cup on a saucer then poured the coffee. Young nodded again, and the butler took a position at the far edge of the patio, keeping us in sight, awaiting further instructions.

"I like to have breakfast out here

whenever the weather cooperates," said Young. "This section of Potrero Hill gets protected from the chilling ocean breezes and provides a nice view of the bay."

"It really is a great view," I said in agreement, scanning the panorama.

"Time to get down to business," Young said, now with a commanding tone in his voice. "Let's have it."

"Yes, sir. My report is right here," I said, pulling the manila envelope from my attaché case and handing it to him.

Young took the envelope. "Please summarize."

"Well, sir," I replied nervously. "You asked me to follow Miss Young to see if she was keeping company with a Mr. Bill Hunter. In the last week, I have tailed her to three rendezvous with him, one in the afternoon and two in the evening, each time at the Palace Hotel. One time, I saw her pay the hotel bill."

Young shook his head, looked down, took in a deep breath, and let it out. "Lisa promised me she had stopped seeing him.

She paid for the hotel?" He took a sip of coffee before continuing. "Well, she gets a sizable allowance."

"I'm sorry, sir. It's all in there: times and photos."

"Thank you, Mr. Malloy," said Young, handing me an envelope and nodding to the butler.

I took that as a signal to leave and stood. "Thank you, Mr. Young."

The butler pointed the way, waving his hand. "This way, sir."

I waited until I was behind the wheel of my car before I opened the envelope. I counted out $250, fifty bucks more than we had agreed on. Nice pay for a week's work, though it would have to cover weeks with no income.

I wanted to clear my tab with Meg. She'd need the money.

Chapter Five

With a pocketful of dough, I was feeling better. Yeah, as good as anyone could feel with a friend laid out in the morgue, a hole in his chest. When I got back to the office, I gave Meg a call to see how she was doing. She invited me to lunch.

The rails on Meg's porch were draped in black. A woman dressed in black answered the door.

"Hello," she said flatly. "You must be Jake; come in."

"Yes, ma'am. Jake Malloy."

"I'm Meg's mother. You can call me Mary. Meg's in the kitchen cooking."

Mary Reilly O' Shay, herself a widow, was a sturdy-looking woman. Her thick black hair was pulled tightly to the back of her head. She was wearing a silver crucifix around her neck. I had no doubt Mary, who had emigrated from Ireland in her early twenties, was supervising the mourning within the house in Irish tradition. The hall mirror had been turned to face the wall. The pendulum on the grandfather clock hung still while the face of the clock read 7:30. We didn't know the exact time of Chuck's death; 7:30 was a reasonable guess.

"This is Liam, Chuck's brother," said Mary. Liam, the older brother, could have been Chuck's twin, save a few gray hairs and some extra weight. He stood and greeted me with a handshake.

Meg, wearing a white apron over her black dress, emerged from the kitchen to greet me. "Hello, Jake."

"*Mo stoirin* (my little darling)," said Mary, walking towards Meg. "Take off your apron and visit. I'll finish in the kitchen."

Meg complied and joined Liam and me around the coffee table, set for tea.

"How are you this morning, Meg?" I asked.

Meg took a deep breath. "Oh, I'm coping. Detective Farrell came by this morning. He asked me a lot of questions about Chuck and the diner. Nothing he asked seemed to make any sense about Chuck getting shot during the robbery."

"I'm sure they were just his standard questions. Doesn't mean anything," I assured her.

"He asked me if I would come downtown for an identification. I told him I did want to see Chuck. I went; it was awful. They had Chuck in a drawer in a basement, more like a dungeon. They rolled out the drawer. He was covered with a sheet. They folded it back enough so I could see his face. 'Is that your husband, Charles Darcy?' Farrell asked. I was able to hold back my tears, just a little, and nod my head. Farrell said, 'Mrs. Darcy, I need you to say it.' Hearing myself saying it was just as tough as getting the words out. 'Yes, that's my husband, Charles Darcy.'"

"Were you able to talk to Farrell about a funeral schedule?"

"Yes, he said the funeral home could get Chuck anytime now. I notified Cooke's. Liam is going to take Mama and me down there after lunch to make the arrangements. Viewing will be Saturday night. St. Bridget doesn't hold funeral services on Sundays, so the funeral will be Monday."

"Should I tell Johnny Kelly to plan the wake for Monday then?" I asked.

"Yes. We'll let Johnny know as soon as the schedule is decided. I want Chuck to have a military funeral. Liam is going to contact the Presidio Army Base to ask for a military honor guard and burial in the national cemetery."

"That's good," I replied. "Chuck deserves those honors."

Mary came out from the kitchen. "Meg, everything's ready. Can you help me get it on the table? You two men can talk on your own."

"Meg says you are a detective. Are you investigating Chuck's murder?" Liam asked.

"I have a one-man agency. I think the

police will be investigating. I'll do what I can. As long as we're on the subject, let me ask you. Did Chuck have any enemies?"

"I don't know."

The next question was one that needed to be asked of someone. Not that I had any suspicions, but affairs sometimes lead to nasty situations. I took advantage of being alone with the brother to ask.

"Look, Liam. It's an insensitive question, I know, but I have to ask. Was there any indication that Chuck was fooling around?"

"Well, to tell you the truth, I haven't seen Chuck in a long time."

"Why's that, if you don't mind me asking?"

"Well, way back, we were both trying to date a girl named Alice, and Chuck won. When I expressed interest in Meg, he dumped Alice for Meg."

"Did you try dating Alice again after that?"

"Yeah, but by then, she was done with the Darcys."

"That's too bad," I said.

Liam shrugged. "A long time ago."

Mary called us to the table. Conversation during the meal was subdued but comfortable. Mary told me about living in Grass Valley, a small town in the Sierra foothills with a working gold mine. Liam talked about his plumbing business across the bay in Walnut Creek. Meg was mostly quiet.

When we were done eating, Mary stood up. "We have to clean up now and get to the undertakers."

I asked Meg if I could talk to her and gave her an envelope. "Meg, you know Chuck let me run a tab at the diner. This should pay it off, and I put in enough to cover next month's rent in advance."

"Thanks, Jake. That's so nice of you."

"I guess I'll be going now. I'll talk with you later," I said.

Meg walked me to the door. "Oh, I almost forgot. We are going to ask Father Duffy to remember Chuck at Sunday's nine o'clock mass," said Meg.

"I'll be there."

CHAPTER SIX

Saturday morning, I woke up with a plan for the day: Looking for a missing cocker spaniel. I got those cases once in a while. The call for this case had come in on Friday when I'd arrived back to the office from Meg's. Unless someone stole the dog, I could usually find it. It didn't take much detective work, nothing an ordinary citizen couldn't do—check the city pound and the SPCA, and post flyers in the neighborhood promising a small reward.

I had gotten my first case by accident one morning at breakfast in the diner. One of Meg's regulars was upset because his dog was missing. I think more as a joke, Meg told the man I was a private detective; he should ask me to find the dog. He did, and I did. He told all his friends, and word of mouth spread of my prowess in dog-finding.

As usual, I had the radio on while I was preparing breakfast. One news report changed the arc of my day.

A man and a woman were shot and killed last night during a robbery attempt at a café on Geary Street. Police say a man, brandishing a gun, confronted the counterman and demanded money. The owner, hearing the commotion, emerged from his office with a pistol. The alleged robber shot at the owner, who returned fire, killing both the gunman and his female companion. The pair is believed to be the Jukebox Bonnie and Clyde robbers who are suspects in the murder of diner owner Chuck Darcy.

I called the precinct; Farrell wasn't in. I asked the desk sergeant to have Farrell contact me about Bonnie and Clyde. While I waited, I prepared a draft of the poster looking for Ruffles, the missing dog. I didn't have to wait long for Farrell to call back. He had already decided he wanted me to come to the morgue to see the bodies.

"Jake, the Bonnie and Clyde robbers

were shot and killed last night during a robbery attempt," Farrell related.

"Yeah, I heard it on the news this morning."

"We've already got two positive IDs from their victims. Can you meet me at the morgue to see if these two are your jitterbug couple?"

"I can be there in forty minutes. Is that okay?" I asked.

"That'll be just fine."

I dressed, and after a quick stop to drop off the Ruffles poster for printing, I drove downtown to the morgue.

***

"Jake Malloy to see Detective Farrell," I told the desk sergeant. He made a phone call, and Farrell arrived in a couple of minutes.

"Good morning, Mike."

"Good morning, Jake. You ready to look at some stiffs?"

"Yeah, no sweat."

Farrell led the way to the "dungeon." The attendant rolled Clyde out first and pulled the sheet off his face.

"I don't know," I said. "I didn't get a good look at his face. He was in the booth next to the jukebox most of the time, then dancing. Could be him."

Farrell nodded. The attendant shoved Clyde back in and rolled Bonnie out. As soon as he lifted the sheet, I could see she wasn't my bobby-soxer. "No. Definitely not her."

"Are you sure?" asked Farrell.

"Yeah, she stood right next to me at the counter—the mouth, the nose, the chin. Not her."

Farrell nodded again; Bonnie went back in the box. "I can't rule them out yet," he said. "They could have arrived after your jitterbug couple left. There's a long time between when you left and our best guess at when Darcy was shot. Clyde had a .38, the same caliber as the slug recovered from Darcy. We're still waiting for ballistics analysis."

"I guess that's it for now. You got any leads?" I asked.

"I do have some stuff I want to show you. Let's go to the conference room."

Farrell picked up an envelope waiting on the conference room table. "I have some copies of the crime scene photos for you." Farrell pulled a photo out and handed it to me. "Look at this one."

"What is this?" I asked.

"It's a blood-stained note on the back of one of Chuck's order sheets. The coroner found it gripped inside Chuck's left hand. We also found a bloody pen under his body."

"I guess I missed the pen when I rolled him over," I said.

"The coroner believes Chuck could have lived for five to ten minutes, bleeding out after being shot. We think he wrote this trying to tell us who shot him."

"With all the dried blood, you can't tell what it says," I commented.

"Yeah, not clear what he wrote. Our forensic guys have been studying it and have a guess. Does the name Melody Jones mean anything to you?"

"Melody Jones! You got Melody Jones out of that? Sounds like a stripper."

"Here, take a look at this marked-up photo," replied Farrell.

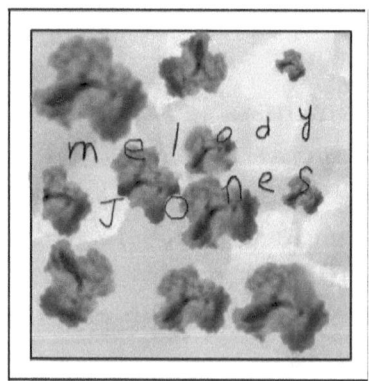

"Yeah, okay. I guess. Who do you think Melody Jones is?"

"Who knows? Maybe your jitterbug girl," replied Farrell. "Anyway, it's the only lead we have now. We've IDed Clyde as Darryl Johnson. Bonnie wasn't carrying any identification. She could be Melody Jones." Farrell returned the photos to the envelope and handed it to me. "I'll let you know if anything new comes up."

I left with the envelope in my hand. The only solid thing that came out of all this was that my jitterbug couple wasn't Bonnie and Clyde. The jitterbug couple were still suspects. Bonnie and Clyde were still suspects until the comparison of the slug that killed Chuck to Clyde's .38 nailed them or cleared them. Maybe Bonnie was Melody Jones, or maybe my bobby-soxer was.

I had one more distressing thought in my head. I hadn't wanted to think Chuck had been having an affair, but could Melody Jones be a jilted lover?

CHAPTER SEVEN

The Sunday 9:00 a.m. mass at St. Bridget was a memorial mass for Chuck. I attended for Chuck, but really more for Meg. Sure, I'm Irish. I was raised in an Irish Catholic household. Did all the things expected of an Irish youth: First Communion, Confirmation, served as an altar boy, even eight years of Catholic elementary school. It had been a long time since I had been to a mass, but I remembered the rituals. Entering, I dipped my hand in the holy water and made the sign of the cross.

Meg had promised that she, her mother, and Chuck's brother would arrive early to sit in the first row, and she'd save a space for me. As I walked to the front of the church, I could see a large contingent from Kelly's was present.

Many of them, I suspected, were hungover. The pews were packed. Meg and her mother were wearing black dresses, and Liam, like me, wore a black suit and tie. The trio slid over to make a space next to Liam. I genuflected, crossed myself, and took my seat.

A memorial mass is a standard mass with all the standing, kneeling, sitting, singing, praying, and the Communion. The only difference is the call for prayers for the dearly departed. Father Duffy switched from his Latin to his Irish brogue for the memorial invocation.

"Today, we pray for the soul of Charles 'Chuck' Darcy, who was so cruelly taken from us Thursday night by the dastardly deed of murder. May God receive him into his kingdom." Duffy looked and indicated with an open hand in Meg's direction. "We pray for his widow and his brother, who sit here in their sorrow but in the belief of everlasting life. Let us pray."

Father Duffy led the congregation in the Lord's Prayer in English, then returned to the Latin liturgy. At the end of the mass, as was standard, Duffy made several announcements. The final announcement called for honoring the grieving family. "We ask the congregation to remain standing and allow the family of Charles Darcy to proceed to the vestibule, where they will receive those who wish to express condolences. A funeral mass will be held tomorrow at one o'clock."

I participated in the small processional up the center aisle to the vestibule, where the three family members took their positions. Not wanting to insert myself in this family function, I stood a few steps behind them, my hands clasped together behind me. I intended to wait until we could leave together. Many, but not all, of the congregants, stopped to talk briefly. Those who didn't want to participate exited the sanctuary via the left or right door.

As people filed by, I studied their faces to see if I could recognize them. Not surprisingly, there were many people I didn't know. After many faces, I started to lose concentration. I was lost in thought when a face startled me to attention. It looked like the jitterbug kid. Then

I saw the girl next to him. It *was* the jitterbug couple!

I casually walked to the front of the group and positioned myself to block the couple's departure. "Hello," I said in a friendly voice.

"Oh, hello," replied the kid. "Weren't you in Chuck's Thursday evening?"

"Yes. And you and your girlfriend were playing the jukebox."

"Uh-huh. We're so sorry. We didn't know Mr. Darcy had been killed. We always attend the 9:00 a.m. mass. This is the first we heard about it. Are you family too?"

The words slid out, "No, just a friend," while I tried to sort out my thoughts. Would the couple expose themselves like this if they were guilty? It could be a clever ruse. No, I didn't think those kids were sophisticated enough to think that way.

"We were just telling Mrs. Darcy how kind her husband was to let us dance in the diner," said the girl.

"Meg, will you excuse us now?" I asked.

"Okay," replied Meg.

"Can you step over here?" I asked the pair while using one arm to gently usher and one arm to point. I showed the couple my P.I. badge. "I'm a private investigator, as well as Chuck's friend. I am going to ask you some questions. Okay?"

"Okay," they both responded nervously.

"When did you leave Chuck's that night?"

"You were there when I got the dollar changed for the jukebox. We put the whole dollar in, played fourteen songs, then left. I don't remember the time," replied the girl.

I had left at six-thirty. Fourteen songs would take maybe thirty minutes, which made it about seven when the jitterbuggers left.

"Was there anyone inside when you left?"

"No."

"Did you see anyone hanging around outside?"

"No."

"Okay. Let me see some ID."

They both produced driver's licenses. I

recorded their names, Gregory White and Linda Soren, and their addresses in my notebook, thanked them, and let them go.

When Meg was ready to go, I asked her if she needed anything from me.

"We'll be okay. Do you want to come back with us for lunch?"

"That would be nice, but I have some things I have to do."

As I walked to my car, I thought about the jitterbug couple and chuckled to myself. *So, she's* not Melody Jones!

***

Back in my office, I checked my answering machine for any messages. The answering machine had been a significant investment for my little detective office. Well worth the two-hundred-dollar price tag, it saved me the expense of a secretary or an answering service. The missing dog posters I hung Saturday evening had done the trick: I had a message, someone claiming to have found Ruffles.

I returned the call. The lady, Mrs. Ray, said she had found the dog wandering in the rain and had brought her inside. I asked Mrs. Ray to describe the dog. When she replied that the dog's tag read Ruffles, I didn't need to hear any more. I asked if I could come right over. She agreed. I took a picture the owner had provided of Ruffles as my bona fides to claim the dog.

After paying the twenty-dollar reward, which I required the client to provide in advance, I claimed the dog and delivered her for a happy reunion of dog and master. I received my fee of twenty five dollars and five dollars for the printing and headed back to the office.

I had solved the missing dog case while the murder case had taken an unexpected turn. I had eliminated the jitterbug couple as suspects. I had only one clue: Chuck's blood-stained note. Who was Melody Jones?

CHAPTER EIGHT

Late Monday morning, I finally reached Farrell. I told him of my encounter with the jitterbug couple and gave him their names and addresses. We both agreed they were probably not involved in Chuck's murder. Still, Farrell said he would check on them. Then Farrell hit me with the news.

"We got the ballistics reports on Clyde's .38. It's definitely not the one that killed Darcy," Farrell reported.

"Looks like the only clue left is the note, Melody Jones," I said.

"Yeah, but we've had no luck finding her. The DMV has no record of a Melody Jones. She's not in the phone book either. We had the phone company check the unlisted numbers too. No dice. We're at a dead end."

"Looks that way, Mike. Hey, I have to go. Leaving for Chuck's funeral now. I'm a pallbearer."

"Goodbye, Jake. Sorry."

"Goodbye, Mike. Thanks."

***

The other pallbearers were sitting quietly in the vestibule when I arrived at Cook's Funeral Home. I recognized four of the five: Johnny Kelly, Chuck's brother, Liam, and two guys from Kelly's. I introduced myself to the fifth.

"I'm Jake Malloy," I said, offering a handshake.

"Lucek Barbinski."

"How do you know Chuck?"

"Chuck and I were in the army together during the war. I haven't seen him since the last reunion of our unit."

"Do you live in the area?

"No. I'm from Kansas City, Missouri."

"Kansas City! How did you hear about Chuck?"

"Another guy from our unit, Tony Bagalio, lives here. He saw the obituary in the paper and contacted me. Tony's in Chuck's military honor guard."

"You and Chuck must have been close for you to come all the way from Kansas City for his funeral."

"When Tony contacted me, he gave me Meg's number. I called her right away and asked if I could be a pallbearer. Meg knew about me and agreed. I had to come. See, Chuck saved my life in Europe."

I was just going to ask Lucek about Chuck saving his life when Father Duffy entered the room. "Good afternoon, boys." Duffy came to each of us, shaking hands and thanking us for volunteering for the ceremony. Duffy knew Kelly and the two bar patrons. Liam, Lucek, and I had to introduce ourselves.

"Now boys, it is a solemn duty you will be performing today. I'm going to give you your instructions now."

After Duffy finished explaining how the casket should be lifted and transported, we all left for the chapel inside the funeral home.

From the back of the chapel where the pallbearers waited, I viewed the silent assemblage. The Irish stoicism was in full force. Duffy walked to the front, stopping to bend and say something to Meg. I could see that she was wearing a black veil over her face.

Chuck's open casket was partially draped with the American flag; the bright red, white, and blue colors were stunning. Meg had decided to bury Chuck in his army uniform with all his combat medals.

Duffy read from the Bible, led the group in prayer, then offered a last goodbye.

Meg and Liam stood. With her left arm entwined in Liam's right, Meg slowly made her way to the open end of the casket. She paused and, after a time, made the sign of the cross. With her trembling black-lace-gloved hand, she patted the olive drab sleeve of Chuck's uniform. Meg's mother and the rest of the congregants followed.

When the last mourner passed, the funeral director closed the casket. The military honor guard ceremonially extended the flag to cover the entire casket. The pallbearers took their places, and the processional started. The honor guard led, followed by the pallbearers pushing the casket-laden gurney, then the three family members and the remaining mourners. The honor guard, consisting of four members, stood two on each side as the pallbearers lifted the casket from the gurney into the hearse.

The funeral caravan drove to St. Bridget's. I was lucky that Meg had some space in the family limo and had invited me to ride with her. That saved me the embarrassment of joining with my old beat-up Studebaker.

We rode in silence until Meg, seemingly unable to hold back her emotions, started weeping quietly, laying her head on her mother's shoulder. As we approached the church, Meg sat straight up, regaining her composure.

At St. Bridget's, the pallbearers carried the casket up the steps to the church using the step-wait method as Duffy had taught us. Inside the vestibule, we placed the coffin on the gurney. The honor guard, with great formality, removed and folded the flag into the traditional triangle shape, the flag not allowed inside the sanctuary.

We slowly wheeled the casket to the front of the church to the mood of the somber organ music. I took notice of the large number of attendees, many of whom I recognized from Kelly's. The others, I guessed, were just friends or acquaintances of Chuck's that I didn't know. Another possibility was that they were strangers attending a veteran's funeral. I had heard some people did that as a remembrance of a loved one killed and buried overseas during the war.

There were three eulogies for Chuck. Father Duffy's focused on Chuck as a family and religious man. Johnny Kelly told how he and Chuck grew up together in San Francisco, telling some funny stories. When Kelly was done, Father Duffy called Lucek to the lay pulpit.

"We will now hear from one of Chuck's brothers-in-arms."

Lucek made his way slowly, carrying a

folded note in his hand. In a quivering voice, he introduced himself. "My name is Lucek Barbinski. Chuck and I were in the army together during the war." The grimace on his face broke with a little smile. "Chuck always called me Lucy.

"Chuck was a hero. He saved my life during the Battle of the Bulge. We were in an artillery observation unit when it got ambushed and captured by the Germans in Belgium. The Nazis decided to massacre the POWs. Somehow, Chuck sensed what was coming and knocked me to the ground. He led, and we crawled to the trees and watched as the rest were machine-gunned. Then a Nazi officer strolled casually through the bodies. He shot anyone still alive or who just looked alive; shot 'em in the head. Because of Chuck, I lived to come home, get married, and have two beautiful children." Lucek started sobbing. "I will never forget him. That's all I have to say."

Despite the Irish stoicism, many handkerchiefs were in use, the most, it seemed, when the soprano sang "Ave Maria."

When the mass was over, the processes were reversed to place the flag-draped casket back in the hearse. The funeral caravan drove to the national cemetery at the Presidio Army Base.

A bagpiper was awaiting our arrival at the cemetery. While we carried Chuck to his final resting place, the piper played "Going Home." We placed the casket on the wooden struts straddling the grave. The honor guard removed the flag and, once again with great formality, folded it into the triangle shape.

Tony Bagalio had been selected to present the flag to Meg. I detected no emotion from Meg, her face covered in a black veil, as Tony presented her with the symbol of Chuck's service. "From a grateful nation."

Father Duffy read several Bible verses, blessed the casket with holy water, then stepped back. The pallbearers took their places and lifted the coffin onto the lowering straps. The funeral crew removed the wooden struts. There were few dry eyes while the bugler played "Taps," and we lowered the coffin into the grave.

"Before we conclude the ceremony, the family has asked me to announce that all are invited to a reception at Kelly's Pub," said Duffy. He moved to a mound of earth at the edge of the grave. Seemingly from nowhere, Duffy produced a small garden shovel and loaded it with earth. Tilting the shovel, he allowed the earth to fall into the grave and atop the casket. "Earth to earth, ashes to ashes, dust to dust."

The piper played "Amazing Grace."

Meg was unsteady as her mother and Liam assisted her to the grave. Liam held Meg's hand and helped her with the shovel to scoop some earth and drop it. Liam and Meg's mother followed with the symbolic burial, then escorted Meg to their limo.

I stayed behind, leaving the family members to themselves. I had told Liam I would catch a ride back with one of the guys from Kelly's.

The gathering thinned as members repeated the earth ceremony and departed; some lingered to talk. The bagpiper played several repeats of "Amazing Grace." When he stopped playing, I left.

The sun was shining.

CHAPTER NINE

After changing my clothes at the office, I walked over to Kelly's, where the wake was in full swing. From a block away, I could hear Kelly's bar band, the Delancy Brothers, playing a traditional Irish protest song, "The Rising of the Moon." To my surprise, a cheer went up when I stepped through the door. Everyone had been waiting for me. Kelly greeted me.

"Jake, you're finally here; time to carry the coffin."

"Coffin! What coffin?" I asked.

Kelly laughed and made a roundup sign, circling his hand above his head. With that, the other pallbearers rose from their seats and joined us. "This way," said Kelly, leading us to his backroom. There he pointed at a rough-hewed wood coffin that had been painted bright green, a portrait of Chuck resting on the top. "This coffin," he said.

"I don't understand," I questioned.

"Well, you see, in the old country, the deceased would be present at the wake, but here we have to bury him first. So we have this stand-in. It's filled with earth from Mother Ireland."

We lifted the heavy coffin. Kelly opened the door and signaled the band. The music stopped. "Follow me," Kelly commanded. We snaked through the crowd and around the barroom as the crowd sang, and the piper played "Oh, Danny Boy." Each man and woman raised their drink as we passed. Finally, we placed the coffin on a two-foot-high platform covered in green felt and positioned at the far end of the bar. All this was new to me.

Kelly started the whiskey tribute by grabbing one of the several bottles of Jameson at that end of the bar and filling one of the many shot glasses also positioned there. Standing in front of Chuck's portrait, he raised his glass in a silent toast, downed the shot, and slammed the glass upside down atop the coffin near the picture. The crowd cheered. The ceremony was repeated by all. When the last person slammed his glass down, Kelly yelled out, "Music!" and the Delancys commenced playing a lively jig. People danced.

The band played and sang many traditional Irish tunes, ballads, protests songs, and jigs. When they tired or, more than likely, the beer-inspired calls of nature forced a break, I decided to take advantage of the relative quiet to talk to Chuck's two army buddies. But first, I had to get some food into my stomach to absorb the alcohol.

The buffet table, covered with traditional Irish foods including stew, shepherd's pie, soda bread, and wake cake, was at the end of the room, far away from the bar. This positioning eliminated interference between those wanting food and those wanting drinks. One dish, called boxty, a kind of potato pancake with meat, was new to me. I filled my plate and looked around for Tony and Lucek.

The brothers-in-arms were sitting together by themselves. "Can I join you?" I asked.

"Sure, have a seat," Tony replied.

"That was a nice service," I said.

"Yeah," replied Lucek. "I am glad I could make it. I've never been to an Irish funeral or wake before. It's really something."

"Me neither," said Tony.

"You like the food?" I asked. They both nodded their satisfaction.

Lucek stood. "I have to hit the latrine, then I'll get another round. You need anything, Jake? Tony and me are doing Guinness and Jameson boilermakers."

"Same for me then."

"So, Tony, had you seen Chuck lately?"

"No, not really. I live across the bridge in Martinez. Don't get into the city much. I did have some business on Market Street six months ago. Stopped into the diner and talked to Chuck a little while he was working. Had a nice burger on the house."

"Did Chuck seem okay?"

"Yeah, sure. Why are you asking?"

"I didn't get a chance to tell you. I am a private detective. I'm working with the police to investigate Chuck's murder."

"I thought he got killed in a robbery."

"That's the way it seems. But we need to investigate all the angles," I replied.

"No, no problems. We talked a little, like I said, while he worked. We were both looking forward to the next reunion a year from now."

"One more question," I promised. "Does the name Melody Jones mean anything to you?

"Nope, never heard that name. Never knew any girl named Melody."

I decided to change the subject. "That was quite a story Lucek told about Chuck saving his life."

"Yeah, that was before I got there. I was a replacement."

Lucek returned with the drinks on a tray: three pints of Guinness and three shots of Jameson's whiskey. Tony, apparently unable to contain his alcohol inspired amusement with me, decided to share it with Lucek.

"Hey Lucy, Jake here is a private dick, and he's looking for a girl." He turned away from Lucek and looked at me. "What was that girl's name?"

"Melody Jones," I answered.

"Melody Jones," Tony repeated, looking at Lucek.

"Never heard of her," said Lucek, shrugging his shoulders and placing the drinks on the table.

Lucek made a toast to Chuck, and we finished off our Jameson in one gulp.

"Lucek, that was a moving story you told, Chuck saving your life."

"I was just telling what Chuck did for me," Lucek said with a shrug.

"I heard a little about the Battle of the Bulge. I was in the Pacific in the Coast Guard during the war. Battle of the Bulge, that was in Belgium?"

"Belgium and France both. December '44, the Germans broke through and created a bulge in our battle lines. We got captured near the Belgium hamlet of Baugnez. The Nazis executed seventy-two guys in my unit. But Chuck and me got away."

"That was horrible," I commented.

"Yeah," said Lucek, grabbing Tony by the shoulder and shaking him. "And new guy here missed all the fun."

"Oh, yeah, sure. Like fighting the rest of the way into Germany was a piece of cake," protested Tony.

At that moment, the band abruptly stopped playing, and the room got quiet. I looked around and could see Kelly at the entrance, waving his right hand and holding his left index finger to his lips. Meg, Liam, and Meg's mother entered. Meg was still in black but without her veil and gloves. The crowd stood in silence as Kelly led the trio to the table reserved for them.

Once he had the group seated, Kelly leaned over and talked with Meg. I saw her nod. Kelly spoke to the band and made an announcement. "The band will now play some of Chuck's favorite Irish tunes."

The band started with "My Wild Irish

Rose" then continued with several songs I didn't know. The crowd sang along and danced. I observed Meg tapping her foot slightly to the beat of some of the jigs.

When the band completed the selected songs, Kelly made another announcement. "At this time, I would like to invite everyone to give a personal tribute to Chuck. Tell us what he meant to you. Tell us a funny story. If you are brave enough or just drunk enough, you can stand on the bar and recite. Mind you now, there are ladies present. Keep it clean."

What followed was a stream of funny, sad, or poignant stories, some raising a raucous response from the well lubricated crowd, some that invoked a smile or laugh from Meg herself.

When story time was over, the band jumped back in. People lined up to converse with Meg. When I got to the front of the line, I greeted Liam and Meg's mother and repeated my condolences to Meg. I apologized for leaving early. "I think I will leave now while I am still able to walk in a straight line. I'll give you a call in the morning."

"I understand, Jake. Be careful walking back," she said. "Thanks for everything."

I made my way back to the office in the dark. Once again, there was no flashing red light from Chuck's sign to welcome me home.

Chapter Ten

I woke up Tuesday morning with a big head that I tried unsuccessfully to cure with aspirin and several cups of black coffee. No alcohol. I had never subscribed to the "hair of the dog that bit you" theory. I decided to skip the morning news on the radio; my brain didn't need any more vibrations. There was nothing on my plate for the day except to call Meg: No lost dogs, no wayward spouses to tail, and no clues to follow in Chuck's murder.

When I felt reasonably alert, I called. Meg picked up after several rings.

"How are you this morning, Meg?"

"I'm okay. How are you?"

"I'm a little hungover, but not too bad," I said.

"Would you like to come over for coffee?" Meg asked. "I have a few things to discuss with you."

"Sure. I'll come right over."

***

The sky, sunny for Chuck's funeral, had returned to the typical San Francisco grey. In the gloom of the morning, it took me much longer than usual to walk the few blocks to Meg's place, my body protesting the exercise.

The black drape on the porch fluttered in the breeze as I climbed the steps to Meg's front door. Meg's mother, still dressed in black, answered my knock.

"Good morning, Jake. Come in."

"Good morning, Mrs. O'Shay."

Meg, also in black, rose from her chair in the parlor and greeted me. "Hello, Jake. Thanks for coming. Please sit here."

I took my seat next to the coffee table, which was prepared with plates of Irish soda bread and wake cake, leftover from the night before, I guessed. In a sweet, gentle voice, Mary O'Shay spoke to Meg. "Mo stoirín, I think the coffee is ready. Can you check?" Once Meg had disappeared into the kitchen, so did the smile on the mother's face. She turned to me, clasped her hands tightly together at waist level, and in a low but stern voice, she advised me. "I want Meg to come back to Grass Valley with me. It won't do her any good to live here where Chuck was murdered. I hope you will encourage her to do so."

"If that's what Meg wants," I replied. "But I think it best if I remain neutral on the subject."

"That will be satisfactory," she replied stiffly.

Meg brought the coffee. Small talk ensued. Meg updated me on some funny stories told at Kelly's after I had left. Her mother remained mostly silent and seemingly unamused. I made no attempt to change the subject, smiling or slightly laughing to reinforce Meg's need to talk about something other than the fallout of Chuck's murder.

When Meg ran out of stories to retell or merely tired of avoiding unpleasant topics, she stopped talking. The silence, waiting for someone to say something, was broken by her mother. "We should get down to business."

Meg sighed. "Yes, Mama."

"Meg is going to come to Grass Valley to live with me," announced her mother, as if spilling a secret.

"Mama, you know I haven't decided yet." Meg turned to me. "Jake, if I do move back to Grass Valley, I intend to sell the diner and this house. The new owner will have to honor the eight months you have remaining on your office lease."

"I understand," I replied. "Don't worry about me. Let me know if there is anything I can help with."

"There is something," replied Meg. "I can't get started on selling the diner until the police release it. The entrance is still marked 'Crime Scene Do Not Enter.'"

"I'll give Detective Farrell a call."

"Thanks." Meg paused for a moment. "Anything new on the investigation?"

I didn't want to depress Meg with the

truth: we were at a dead end. "I think Farrell is working on a few leads." The time had come, and it looked like the best time to ask Meg about Melody Jones. Meg was the only one left to ask. At the wake, Liam had denied any knowledge of the mystery woman. Letting the chips fall where they may, I had to let Melody Jones out of the bag. "We are trying to find a woman named Melody Jones."

Meg's mother shot back quickly, leaving Meg no time to reply. "And what do you think this woman has to do with Chuck?"

"We don't know," I said with a shrug, trying to appear casual. "It's just a name on a slip of paper we found on the floor in the diner," I replied, sugar-coating the truth. "Maybe somebody else was looking for her, and Chuck just wrote down the name. Maybe she was there that night and saw something. Just something to look into."

Meg was staring at me, maybe through me, expressionless. "I've never heard that name," she said quietly.

The glare on Mary O'Shay's face was

giving me third-degree burns; it was time to leave. "Okay," I replied. "I guess I should be going." I gulped down the rest of my coffee and stood.

My escape was delayed when Meg insisted that I take some of the leftover soda bread and wake cake. "Jake, you should take some cake to your office."

"No, no, thanks. You should keep it for other visitors."

"We've got plenty. Mama, can you wrap a couple of pieces for Jake? The wax paper is in the drawer next to the tableware."

When her mother disappeared into the kitchen, Meg leaned over towards me and whispered, "You don't think Chuck and this woman—?"

I interrupted her before she could finish the question. "No, there's no evidence of anything like that."

Meg leaned back. "Good."

Meg's mother returned, and without saying a word, handed the bag of cakes to Meg.

"Thanks, Mama." Meg passed the bag to

me. "Here you are, Jake." Meg walked me to the door.

"I'll call Farrell about releasing the diner as soon as I get back to the office."

"Thanks, Jake."

When I passed Kelly's, I was tempted to stop.

I kept going.

Chapter Eleven

On my walk home from Meg's, I got hit by rain. I was soaked by the time I reached the office, and despite my effort to save it by stuffing it under my trench coat, the brown paper bag of Irish baked goods was mush. The cakes were just fine. Despite Mary O'Shay's newfound animosity towards me, she'd done a perfect job of wrapping the cakes in wax paper. I had eaten enough cake for the day and saved them for the next two days' breakfast.

After changing into dry clothes and hanging my wet things all over the office to dry, I called Farrell. I was lucky he was at his desk.

"Detective Farrell."

"Mike, it's Jake."

"Jake, I was just going to call you."

"What for?"

"Well, you called me," replied Farrell. "Why don't you go first?"

"Okay. I was talking to Meg Darcy this morning. She's anxious to get back into the diner. She may sell and move home with her mother. She wants to know when you'll release the diner as a crime scene."

"I understand. It should only be a few more days. I may send the forensic guys back in for another look."

"I'll let her know. Now, what's on your mind?"

"Do you know a guy named Lucek Barbinski?"

"Sure. He's a friend of Chuck's. He was a pallbearer at the funeral yesterday."

"He's dead," said Farrell. "A patrol car found him near the corner of Anglo Alley and Pacheco Street about one o'clock this morning. Shot with a .38."

"I can't believe it! He was in town just for the funeral."

"It looks like a robbery. We found his

wallet dumped on the sidewalk next to his body, no cash. No cash in his pockets. We found your card in his wallet."

"Yeah, I talked to him last night at Kelly's pub where we had Chuck's wake. That corner is just two blocks from Kelly's."

"What do you know about him?"

"Not much. Just met him at the funeral. He was from Kansas City, Missouri, married, two kids. He and Chuck were in the army together during the war, close buddies."

"I see a Kansas City address on his driver's license. I can get the local police to notify the widow. Sometimes it's better if a friend does the notification. Do you have the phone number?"

"No. And like I said, I just met him. One of Chuck's other army buddies, Tony Bagalio, lives in the area. I think they were all close. He might be willing to make the call."

"Okay," said Farrell. "See if Bagalio will call. I'll hold off until three. If I haven't heard from you by then, I'll get the cops in Kansas City to handle it."

"I'll get right on it and let you know," I replied, and hung up.

***

Tony owned and operated an auto repair shop in the small town of Martinez across the Oakland Bay bridge. I got him on the phone just past noon.

"Tony, this is Jake Malloy. We met at Chuck's funeral."

"Oh, yeah, Jake. I remember you. "What's up?"

"I got bad news. Lucek is dead. Shot sometime last night."

"I can't believe it!" responded Tony. "We were supposed to get together for dinner tonight. He was going home tomorrow morning. What happened?"

"The cops found him early this morning, dead on the sidewalk two blocks from Kelly's. Looks like a robbery; all his cash was gone."

"That's terrible."

"I'm sorry. When's the last time you saw Lucek?"

"I called it quits at midnight. I had to

drive back to Martinez—the shop opens at seven. Lucek said he was going to stay a little longer. That's something. Chuck and Lucek survived the war and came home to get killed in robberies."

"I'm going to level with you. I don't think these were robberies. I think your two buddies were intentionally murdered."

"But why would someone want to kill Chuck and Lucek?"

"I was wondering if you had any idea," I replied.

"Got no idea. They were real good guys."

"Look, Tony. Something's going on here. Two guys with nothing in common, except being in the army together, get murdered within a couple of days. You served with them. Is there something in their army experience to motivate murder?"

"I swear there is nothing like that," replied Tony.

"Are you sure?"

"I'm sure."

"And you never heard of Melody Jones?"

I asked.

"Never! Why do you keep asking?"

"The cops think she's involved in Chuck's murder," I responded.

After a period of silence, Tony replied firmly, "Well, I don't know her."

"Okay. I'm going to ask you a favor. Do you know Lucek's wife?"

"Joan? Sure. I met her at the last reunion. Me and my wife had dinner with her and Lucek."

"Someone has to notify her of Lucek's death. The cops think it better if she heard it from someone she knows. Can you do it?"

"Okay, I can do it."

"Thanks. Mike Farrell is the lead detective; you can reach him at Klondike 5-1018. Give Mrs. Barbinski his number, and mine too."

After I hung up, I called Farrell's office and left a message informing him Tony would talk to our new widow. Needing a drink—not for "hair of the dog," just in general—I went to Kelly's.

***

"Hey, Jake, how are you feeling this fine day?" Kelly greeted me.

"Okay, now. Not so good this morning," I replied. "I'll have a Guinness."

Kelly slowly filled a pint mug from the tap, and without looking up, he asked, "Did you hear about the body they found down the street last night?"

Nodding and taking a sip, I replied. "Yeah, he was one of Chuck's pallbearers. Lucek, the one who spoke at his funeral."

"Oh, God, no! That was him?" Kelly made the sign of the cross over his body.

"Yeah. The cops called me this morning. He had my card on him."

"Robbery? It's been pretty safe around here for a long time."

"Yeah, looks like a robbery. He had no cash on him. The cops found his empty wallet next to the body."

"It's a terrible thing," said Kelly, shaking his head.

"Yeah," I agreed.

"I'll say some prayers for him on Sunday."

"Good," I replied.

Kelly shook his head. "Hey, are you hungry? I've got a pot of leftover stew warming in the kitchen."

"That would be great. Thanks."

After finishing a bowl of Irish stew and a second pint of Guinness, I went back to my office.

CHAPTER TWELVE

I wasn't exactly bright-eyed and bushy-tailed Wednesday morning, after a restless night with the two murders bouncing around in my brain. It was the time of the year when the morning sun streamed through my office window onto my desk. The sun warmed my back as I sat in my swivel chair, having a breakfast of black coffee and leftover Irish cakes.

Lucek's murder got four lines on page seven of the morning edition of the *San Francisco Chronicle*. Nothing on the radio; old news to them. I was pondering the scenarios. There were two possibilities.

Case One—The two murders were just weirdly coincidental; a robbery, and a robbery that went wrong.

Case Two—The two murders were linked somehow, maybe by the mysterious Melody Jones. Possibly by victims' military service.

One thing was for sure; both men were shot with a .38. Ballistic comparison of the slugs might point in the right direction. I needed to call Farrell.

"Mike, this is Jake. Anything on the Darcy and Barbinski bullets?"

"Just got the report. No good—the Barbinski bullet was too damaged for striation analysis to compare to the Darcy bullet."

"That doesn't help at all," I said. "You got any ideas?"

"I'm going with robbery on both guys. I contacted the Robbery Division. They report two recent robberies in the area, no shooting; both victims gave similar descriptions. They thought the robber brandished a .38."

"What did the guy look like?" I asked.

"You know how good witness info is. What I got was medium height, medium build, Caucasian, wearing a raincoat and a knit hat."

"Can't do much with that."

"Nope. Hey, some cases never get solved," replied Farrell.

"Sure, Mike. I know that. Anything more on Melody Jones?"

"Nope, nothing."

"Their murders could be linked by their military service. Maybe it's worth looking into."

"I don't buy it. It's grasping for straws, and I've got too many open cases to run down a blind alley."

"I'll take it," I replied. "Barbinksi told a story about him and Darcy and a Nazi massacre during the Battle of the Bulge. Might be more to it than he let on. I know what military outfit they were in. I'm going to start there."

"Battle of the Bulge, huh? I know just the guy you should talk to, Professor Olaf Linstrom at the University of San Francisco. He's the local expert on the history of the war. I took a course from him last year when I was working on finishing my college degree. He knows his stuff."

"That's great. Do you have a number for

Linstrom?" I asked.

"No. Just contact the history department and ask for him."

"Thanks, Mike. I'm going to call right now."

***

I got the number of the history department and called. The secretary answered.

"History department, Miss Samson."

"Hello, Miss Samson. My name is Jake Malloy. I am trying to reach Professor Linstrom."

"Let me check his schedule.... Doctor Linstrom is in class right now. Can I take a message?"

"Can you ask him to call me? Jake Malloy, Klondike 5-1118."

"Are you one of his students?"

"No. I'm researching an incident during the Battle of the Bulge. I'm hoping I can get some insight from him."

"Needs insight into the Battle of the Bulge," Samson repeated. "Okay, I will leave the message for him. He teaches until twelve.

He may go to lunch after that. Not sure when he will see this."

"Okay. Thanks, Miss Samson."

So, I got stuck waiting for Linstrom to return my phone call. I spent the time cleaning my snub-nosed .38 shoulder piece and my Colt Pocket .32 that I carried in my ankle holster. I was halfway through a thorough cleaning of my office when the phone rang.

"Jake Malloy."

I was surprised when I didn't hear Linstrom's voice on the other end.

"Malloy, this is Carl Young," said the voice on the other end. Young, the rich guy who had hired me to tail his daughter to her liaisons with her boyfriend, the fortune hunter, as Young described him.

"Yes, Mr. Young. Good afternoon."

"Malloy, I am in need of more of your services. Can you come to the house this afternoon?"

"Yes, sir. What time?"

"Three?"

"Okay. Can you tell me what it's about?"

I asked.

"Let's just wait until you get here," Young replied.

"Yes, sir. See you then."

I hardly had time to guess what new job Young might have for me when the phone rang again.

"Jake Malloy."

"Mr. Malloy, this is Dr. Linstrom. I have a note here that says you want to talk to me about the Battle of the Bulge."

"Yes, sir. Thanks for calling. I'm a private investigator. I'm looking into the recent murder of two army buddies that were in the Battle of the Bulge. They both survived a Nazi massacre at a place, not sure how to say it—I think it's pronounced Bag-ney—in Belgium."

"Oh, yes. I am very familiar with that incident. You are pronouncing it correctly. It's spelled B-A-U-G-N-E-Z. Sorry to hear two of our veterans have been murdered. I will be happy to talk to you. Do you know the name of the unit they were in?"

"385th Field Artillery Observation

Battalion."

"Good. That would be helpful to learn how they were involved in the battle. I can give you a little time tomorrow afternoon. One-thirty?"

"Yes, sir. Thanks."

***

The butler answered my ring at Young's Potrero Hill mansion.

"Welcome back, Mr. Malloy. This way, please. Mr. Young is waiting for you in the library." The door to the library was open; the butler announced me. "Sir, Mr. Malloy."

"Send him in," replied Young. He pointed to a chair. "Coffee?" he asked.

"No. Thanks." I waited for him to start the conversation.

"I called you here because I'm not sure my daughter has stopped seeing this guy, Bill Hunter."

"Do you want me to start a new tail?"

"No. I need to convince this guy that he will never get access to my money. I've told my daughter if she marries him, I will disinherit her immediately, and she will receive no further support from me. I want you to convey that message to him."

"I can do that."

"There's something else." Young reached for a business-sized envelope on his side table and passed it to me. "Here's a check for $10,000 made out to Bill Hunter. I want you to give it to him and tell him to leave my daughter alone."

"You want to buy him off," I replied.

"That's right. And when I get the canceled check back, I will show it to my daughter to prove Hunter is only interested in money."

"Got it. Anything else?"

"No, that's it."

I stood up. "I will try to get this done tonight."

CHAPTER THIRTEEN

Back at the office, I prepared for my meeting with Hunter. I always carried my shoulder piece when I was on a job. Even off the job, I was rarely without it. Snooping around and tailing someone from a distance was one thing. Getting face-to-face in a contentious situation was another. For scenarios that posed additional danger, I preferred to carry my Colt Pocket .32 in an ankle holster as a backup. I had practiced and maintained proficiency in drawing from the ankle holster from all three possible positions: standing, sitting, and laid out on the floor. I loaded the .32 and strapped it to my right ankle, and left to find Hunter.

***

My first job for Young had been tailing

his daughter, Lisa, to find out who she was seeing without his permission. That's when Bill Hunter came into the picture. Young then asked me to investigate Hunter. I hadn't been able to dig up much on him. I'd pegged him in his mid-forties. He didn't have any detectable source of income. He spent many daytime hours in Demici's, an Italian coffee house, and evenings in Dorfman's Brauhaus. I had schmoozed his landlady to learn Hunter had been in his apartment for less than a year. None of his neighbors admitted knowing him.

In the afternoon or early evening, depending on how you looked at it, I set out to contact Hunter, guessing I would find him in the coffee house or the beer hall. I tried the coffee house first, but no dice. I had promised Young I would take care of things that night. My preference was to confront Hunter in a public place and not be forced to go to his apartment. I was hoping I would find him in the Brauhaus.

Dorfman's occupied a large space, worthy of its description as a beer hall. A sturdy, bearded man was tending the long bar on the left, where men stood with firm grips on their beer mugs. Tables occupied the center of the room. Booths that could accommodate six people lined the wall to the right. The bar, the booths, and the chairs were all made of wood matching the dark wood of the walls. Hand-painted beer steins and German coats of arms were displayed throughout the hall. At the end of the room, a cuckoo clock hung from the wall. The single waitress visible wore a traditional Bavarian dress with a bodice that enhanced her décolletage.

I scanned the room as I walked to an open section of the bar. The tables were empty, but some of the booths were occupied. There was no sight of Hunter. I decided to order a beer, maybe some food, and wait for a while. The bartender came to take my order.

"What'll yah have?"

"Hefeweizen and a menu."

The bartender plopped a menu in front of me and moved to the taps. I was scanning the list of dishes featuring a variety of German sausages when the cuckoo began announcing six o'clock. The cuckooing brought my attention to the end of the room, and I detected some movement in the last booth. I had to spin around again for the bartender.

"Here's your beer, sir. That'll be one dollar."

I put a buck on the bar and took a sip from the glass mug to lower the full head of beer to below the top of the glass. With the beer mug in my left hand, leaving my right hand, my gun hand, free, I took a stroll towards the end of the room, pretending to admire the wall decorations. When I got to a point where I could get a full look into the last booth, I saw, without a doubt, Hunter sitting as close to the wall as possible. I was there to talk to him, so beer in hand, I casually approached him.

Before I could get close, he called out to me. "Good evening, Mr. Malloy. Please join me."

"Okay," I replied, a little off-balance, and slid into the booth, sitting across from him.

"You are surprised that I know who you are," he said.

"Yeah, I am."

"I've been aware of you for a while now; you have been following Lisa and me. Lisa found one of the bills you sent to her father. Once I understood someone was tailing us, I kept an eye out, spotted you a couple of times."

"I guess I'll have to work on my shadowing techniques."

"I guess you're right. So tell me, Mr. Malloy. Why are you here?" asked Hunter.

"I've been looking for you to deliver a message from Carl Young."

"Oh, yeah? So, what's the message?"

"Mr. Young wants you to stay away from Lisa. He's got this idea that you're only interested in her to get to his money."

"But we are in love," Hunter protested, in a way I thought insincere.

"Mr. Young is dead set against Lisa being with you. If she keeps seeing you, he will cut off her allowance and disinherit her. Is your love strong enough to get by without Young's money?"

Hunter paused before answering as if he

was contemplating his dilemma. "Well, that's an interesting question, isn't it?"

"Young wants to help you with your decision." I reached into the breast pocket of my coat, pulled out the envelope Young had given me, placed it on the table, and pushed it to Hunter.

Hunter picked up the envelope and pulled out the check. "A check for $10,000," he announced. Holding the check in his right hand, he rubbed his chin with his left hand.

"Do we have an agreement?" I asked.

"Sure. Why not?" he answered with a smile. "Love can only go so far."

"All right," I said, nodding. "I will inform Young that you have accepted." I stood up, grabbing my beer in my left hand. "Good evening. I hope we don't have to meet again."

"Good evening, Malloy," Hunter replied pleasantly.

I returned my nearly full beer mug to my place at the bar. The bartender asked me if I was going to order food. "No, I'm not hungry now," I replied and left.

When I got back to the office, I called Young and told him Hunter had accepted the check and the deal.

CHAPTER FOURTEEN

The University of San Francisco, founded by the Society of Jesus, the Jesuits, dated back to 1855. Anchored at one corner by St. Ignatius Church (c. 1914), the Fulton Street campus, established in 1930, was a mix of older and newer buildings. The church's twin steeples were visible from almost everywhere on the grounds, providing a reference point for navigating the campus. I made my way to the history department, following Miss Samson's instructions. "From the church go north three buildings, then turn right past two buildings to Beekman Hall. We're on the second floor."

If I hadn't already known USF was a Jesuit and male-only institution, I might have guessed from walking across the campus.

The pedestrian traffic was all conservatively dressed men, with Jesuit priests in traditional robes mingled in. Some of the students were of the usual college age, right out of high school. Many were more mature, reflecting the ex-GIs taking advantage of the post-war GI Bill educational benefits. I, myself, had attended P.I. school using those benefits.

The door to the history department was open. Miss Samson greeted me. "Good afternoon. May I help you?"

"Good afternoon. I'm Jake Malloy. I have an appointment with Dr. Linstrom."

"Oh, yes, Mr. Malloy. I remember. I know he's expecting you. Third door on the left," she said, pointing down the faculty corridor.

Linstrom's door was open. A white-haired man wearing a gray long-sleeved shirt and a blue tie was sitting, hunched over, and reading behind a desk covered with piles of books and papers. Because of his civilian dress, I assumed him to be a lay faculty member.

I knocked, leaning into the doorway. "Dr. Linstrom, Jake Malloy."

"Yes, yes." He stood for a handshake, then gestured to a chair. "So, you want to know about the Baugnez incident during the Battle of the Bulge?"

"Yes, sir. As I told you over the phone, I'm a private investigator." I flashed my P.I. badge and ID. "Last Thursday, a friend of mine, Chuck Darcy, was killed in his diner. It looked like a holdup. He was ex-army and may have tried to fight back. I've been investigating, in coordination with the police. Not much luck. During his funeral, one of his out-of-town army buddies, Lucek Barbinski, told a story of the two of them surviving the massacre at Baugnez. Early Tuesday morning, Barbinski was found shot dead in what looks like another robbery; all his cash was gone."

"And you think their murders are connected to their army experiences, particularly Baugnez?"

"The police detective I work with thinks I'm grasping for straws, but we don't have much else."

"Well, you are lucky. I was the official

historian assigned to the staff of General Omar Bradley from D-Day to Germany's surrender. I have checked my files and notes, and indeed units of the 385th group were at Baugnez. What's the story Barbinski told?"

"The two of them were able to hide before the Nazis started shooting. They saw an officer go through the bodies and execute anyone still alive."

"That's consistent with the stories told by other survivors," replied Linstrom. "There's a couple of other things you should know. Baugnez wasn't the only massacre that day, December 17, 1944. There was an earlier massacre at Büllingen, both sites near the town of Malmedy. In 1946, there was a trial for seventy-three Nazis, many sentenced to death. No executions have been carried out yet, while those cases are still in review. Some perpetrators may still be on the loose."

"So, it looks like Barbinski's story could be true," I said.

"Yes. There's one more thing. There may have been cases of American G.I.s killing

German POWs in revenge."

"Sorry to hear that," I said.

"That's the general history of those Battle of the Bulge massacres," Linstrom said, handing me a bulky manila envelope. "I can lend you this copy of an extensive report on the incidents if you like."

"Thanks, yes," I replied.

"Then sign this receipt. I expect it back in two weeks. Do you mind if I see your driver's license?"

I signed for the report while Linstrom copied my address from my license.

***

Back at the office, I tossed Linstrom's envelope on my desk and checked my answering machine. I had one message from David Miller, a lawyer that I had helped with a divorce case, saying he had a job for me. It was too late in the day for me to reach him. Whatever the job was, I had to take it. I needed the income. My meeting with Linstrom had provided a degree of credibility to Lucek's story but nothing new to work on. I was ready to agree with Farrell that the case might never be solved. I knew I had to get back to work and planned to call the lawyer first thing the next morning.

Needing a drink, I grabbed the bottle of Jameson I kept in the bottom drawer of my desk and poured myself two fingers. The most comfortable place to sit in my office was a big stuffed armchair. I plopped myself down and began sipping my whiskey, just staring, trying to relax my mind. I had a nice view across my desk, out the window to the sky and the tops of the buildings across the street.

Something started to click in my head. There were two envelopes on my desk, Linstrom's and the one containing the crime scene photos Farrell had given me. I stood up, my mind racing. I sat at my desk, opened Linstrom's envelope, and read the report title. "Malmedy Massacre and Trials."

I opened Farrell's envelope and took out the photos of the blood-stained note, the original and the one indicating Melody Jones.

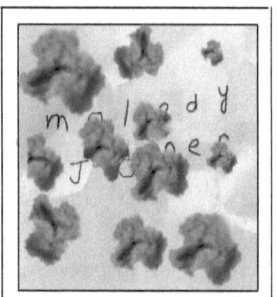

In my desk, I kept some tracing paper I used to check for forged signatures. I grabbed a sheet and put it over the original photo, and traced a new interpretation of the note.

Malmedy! Not Melody. That's why we could never find Melody Jones. There never was a Melody Jones. Chuck was trying to tell us his killer was linked to the Malmedy

Massacres. The second word in the note could still be Jones, but I wasn't willing to accept that so quickly again. I didn't know what to do with this new lead. I tried to contact Farrell, but I couldn't reach him. I needed to calm down. It was Thursday. Kelly allowed an amateur Irish band to play on Thursday nights. Everybody would join in singing. That's something that I needed that night. I headed for Kelly's.

CHAPTER FIFTEEN

Friday morning, I called Farrell. "Mike, I got some news."

"Oh, yeah. What is it?"

"First, can you get out the Darcy crime scene photos, the ones of the blood-stained note?"

"Okay. Got'em."

"I talked with Professor Linstrom yesterday. Do you remember me telling you how Darcy and Barbinski survived a massacre during the Battle of the Bulge?"

"Yeah."

"Linstrom said there were several massacres the same day, all near the Belgian town of Malmedy."

"So?"

"Look at the original photo. You guys interpreted the first word as Melody. I think it's really Malmedy spelled m-a-l-m-e-d-y. I used tracing paper over the copy you gave me. It fits."

"I guess I can see that," responded Farrell. "Are you thinking there never was a Melody Jones?"

"That's what I think. Darcy's killer must have something to do with Malmedy. That's what Chuck was trying to say."

"I can buy it. And the second word? You still going with Jones?"

"I think we should hold off on the Jones for a while, see if anything else pops."

"Okay, what now? I'm still leaving this in your lap."

"I'm not sure. I may talk with Tony Bagalio in Martinez again. He might know some other guys who were in Belgium with Darcy and Barbinski."

"Good luck with that. Let me know if you get anywhere or need anything."

"Okay, Mike, will do."

***

I returned the call from Miller, the lawyer, and got my assignment, a P.I.'s bread and butter job: trailing and photographing a husband suspected of philandering. His wife wanted to check if he was really spending his Saturday mornings playing golf. Miller gave me the address and told me the guy usually left his house around 8:00 a.m. I was to keep tabs on him until he got back home.

"Get some photos, prove where he went, one way or the other," Miller had directed.

"Yes, sir. Will do."

***

The last thing on my plate that morning was to talk with Meg. I knew it would be tough to tell her Chuck's murder might involve something other than a robbery. I had to clear up any thoughts she might have of Chuck's relationship to the nonexistent Melody Jones. Her mother needed to know too. I would leave that job to Meg. I called, and Meg invited me over.

Meg, in black—she'd be in black for

the traditional one year—greeted me with a friendly but subdued smile. We sat for coffee. I inquired how she was doing.

"Okay. Things have settled down. People have stopped bringing cakes and casseroles. This is the last of the cake," she said, passing a slice to me. "I have decided to sell and move to Grass Valley. Can't get started with the diner yet. The cops still have me locked out."

"Oh, I'm sorry," I replied. "I'll call Detective Farrell again and ask him when the diner will be released. Maybe you should call him yourself. He might be more sympathetic if you ask him. Do you have his phone number?"

"Yes. He left his card."

"Meg, there's something I need to tell you. It concerns Melody Jones." Meg tensed up when she heard the name again. "We now believe there never was a Melody Jones."

"I don't understand," she said. "I thought there was some note with her name on it."

"That's kind of true. There was a note next to Chuck's body, but it was hard to read." I was still trying to sugarcoat it as much as possible. "The cops decided it said Melody Jones, but some new information has changed my mind on what it said."

"New information?" she asked.

"Yes. Do you remember that story Lucek told at the funeral mass, Chuck saving his life from the Nazi massacre?"

"Yes, I remember," she replied.

"Well, I have done some investigating, and I found that event was just one of several incidents the same day near the Belgium town of Malmedy. Later, they were all lumped together as the Malmedy Massacres. We think the note Chuck left said Malmedy, not Melody."

Meg put her head down for a moment, then looked back at me. "So, you think someone killed Chuck on purpose, something to do with Malmedy?"

"Yes. And that may tie Chuck's and Lucek's deaths together. They were both survivors of the same Malmedy Massacre. What originally looked like two different holdup-related killings may be linked to the massacre."

"Does that help your investigation any?"

she asked.

"The only thing I can think of is to talk with Tony again. He wasn't in the unit with Chuck and Lucek during the Battle of the Bulge, but he attends the reunions. He might know someone with knowledge of the massacre and aftermath."

"I see," she replied.

It hadn't occurred to me before, but it did then. I needed to ask Meg. "Did Chuck ever talk about it, the massacre?"

"It's strange. If you had asked me that question a week ago, I would have said no. But yesterday, I was going through Chuck's things, starting to get ready for my move to Grass Valley. I found the box where Chuck kept some of his army stuff — medals, purple heart — and I started to remember. Chuck never liked to talk about his combat experience. He liked to tell funny stories about him and his buddies, but not the combat."

"I think many ex-GIs are like that; don't like to talk about it," I said.

"I knew he'd been wounded. I could

see the scar on his shoulder. One night, he was drunk and started telling stories about D-Day. I asked him if that was when he got the wound. He said yes, and that was the closest he ever came to getting killed. Then he corrected himself and told the story of him and Lucek escaping the Nazi massacre of POWs."

"Anything different than what Lucek told at the funeral?" I asked.

"There is one thing; Chuck said he thought he recognized the Nazi officer who went through the bodies. Somebody he had chauffeured before he entered the service."

"That's incredible!"

"I found it hard to believe, but I let it go. Chuck was drunk."

"Did Chuck mention a name?"

"Best I can remember, something like Younger or Young," Meg replied. "Can you do anything with that?"

"Maybe. It seems farfetched, but I am going to go with it for a while. Young and Younger are common names." I replied. There were probably hundreds of Youngs in the

San Francisco phone book and hundreds of thousands in the country. The fact one of those Youngs was a client didn't have the strength of probability to ring any of my bells. "There may be something in the chauffeur angle. Do you know where he worked as a chauffeur?"

"No. That was before I knew him."

We chatted some more. I asked Meg to tell me about the Grass Valley area. I hadn't said anything to Meg, but when she mentioned Chuck's chauffeuring, I remembered Kelly's story, how he lost the chauffeuring job to Chuck. When I left Meg, I headed to Kelly's.

CHAPTER SIXTEEN

I got to Kelly's just past noon. The Friday lunch crowd was small but boisterous. Johnny Kelly was nowhere in sight—Tommy Bannigan was tending the bar. Shannon, whose real name was Ethel, was running orders from the tables to and from the bar and the kitchen.

"Hi, Tommy," I said, taking a seat at the bar. "Johnny in today?"

"Nah, he's not in yet. Today's Friday. He stays open late on Friday nights, so he doesn't show until twelve-thirty. I opened up for him at eleven."

"I need to talk to him, so I guess I'll wait. I'll take a Guinness and a shot of Jameson's… and a corned beef sandwich."

"You got it," replied Tommy. He wrote

my sandwich order down on a slip of paper, took it into the kitchen, and returned to serve my drinks.

I threw the shot down and sipped on my beer, intending to save a few ounces to go with my sandwich. A beer and a shot were all the booze I was going to allow myself when I didn't know what lay ahead in the day. Kelly must have come in the back way, as he appeared suddenly behind the bar. He greeted me with a big grin.

"Hey, Jake. How you been?"

"So, so. I need to talk with you about Chuck."

Kelly dropped the grin. "Okay. What?"

"It's a little noisy here. Can we go to your office?" I asked.

"Sure," replied Kelly. "Tommy, I'll be in my office for a while."

I swigged the rest of my beer, left half a sandwich on the plate, and followed Kelly to his office.

Kelly sat behind his desk, me in a hardback straight chair. "What about Chuck?

You got something new on his murder?" he asked.

"Yep. Do you remember the story Lucek told at the funeral, how Chuck saved him from the Nazi massacre?"

"Sure."

"I've been investigating, and I think Chuck and Lucek's murders may have something to do with the massacre. I was just talking with Meg, and she now remembers Chuck telling the story about it. He told her he thought the Nazi officer who executed the survivors was someone he had driven when he was chauffeuring."

"Wow, that's disturbing," Kelly responded.

"You said Chuck got hired instead of you for the job. Do you remember who he drove for?"

"Yeah. Chuck was hired by Pacific Limousines. He did most of his driving for the German Consulate."

"Germany had a consulate here in San Francisco?"

"Yeah, that was before the war. The consulate was on O'Farrell just off Market."

"And Chuck was okay driving Germans?"

"Look, you don't know how things were around here back then. When did you come to Frisco?"

"I got here in the fall of '42 with the Coast Guard," I replied.

"So, let me tell yah. Me and Chuck graduated from high school in 1938. Work was hard to find, with the Depression still going. When Chuck took the job with Pacific, he didn't know he'd be driving Germans. He didn't mind, at first. San Francisco had a large population of German immigrants. There wasn't a lot of anti-German sentiment, even after a bunch of them started supporting Hitler because he was rebuilding Germany. Hell, the mayor had a reception for the Germans, flew the Nazi flag right next to the Stars and Stripes in City Hall. So, you shouldn't be judging Chuck for working for the Germans."

"Sorry. I was just surprised."

"Yeah, that's okay."

"Do you know who he drove?" I asked.

"We'd get together once in a while, and he'd tell me about his job. He drove all kinds of guys from the consulate and big wigs that came to Frisco to beat the drum for Hitler. The Germans had this U.S. organization called the German American Bund or Federation. Chuck always drove when one of those guys came in."

"Do you remember any names?"

"No," Kelly replied, shaking his head.

"Maybe Young or Younger?

"Nope."

"And Chuck never expressed concerns that he was driving for the Germans or had any problems with them?"

"Things were okay until the war started in Europe. Then the anti-German, anti-Nazi sentiment started to grow. Chuck needed the job and hung in there."

"How long did Chuck drive for them?" I asked.

"Until January, '41. So, the war in Europe was a year and a half old."

"Do you know why he left?"

"I remember. It was a big deal. Chuck was driving to the consulate one day to pick up a passenger, and he couldn't get anywhere near the building. A crowd of thousands of people had jammed the street protesting a huge Nazi flag. Two American sailors from a ship at Mare Island managed to climb up the building and tear the flag down, cheered on by the crowd. Chuck told Pacific Limos he wouldn't drive the Germans anymore. He got fired that day."

"That's quite a story. Anything else?" I asked.

"No. That's all I remember. Does that help?"

"Maybe. I'll have to look into this German consulate thing. Don't know what I'll be looking for."

Kelly and I went back to the bar. "One on the house?" Kelly asked.

"No thanks, Johnny. I've had enough for a while. I might be back later. What band you got coming in tonight?"

"The Irish Rogues."

"Oh, I like them," I replied. "Take it

easy."

"You too, Jake."

***

When I got back to the office, I called Gary Winston, my contact at the *San Francisco Chronicle*. Gary had been working at the paper for over thirty years. Not much of the goings-on in the city could escape Gary.

"Hey, Gary. This is Jake Malloy."

"Hello, Jake. You must be on a case. That's the only time you call me."

"Well, you know how it is."

"Yeah, I know how it is. What is it this time?" he asked.

"I need to do some digging into the German consulate that was on O'Farrell Street before the war."

"I can help you with that. I'm real busy today. Why don't you come down to the paper tomorrow, say three o'clock?"

"Great! Thanks. See you then," I replied.

"Okay, Jake. And you're going to owe me a couple of beers."

"That's okay with me."

CHAPTER SEVENTEEN

I was up early Saturday morning for my job trailing McCandless. He was supposed to leave his house for the golf course around eight. I got to his Pacific Heights neighborhood at seven-thirty and spotted his car parked in front of his Victorian mansion. Luckily, I found a parking spot for my old Studebaker where I could keep an eye on McCandless' late-model Cadillac. McCandless left his house at 8:04. I snapped a couple of pictures of him getting into his car, then followed him loosely to the Golden Gate golf course.

I got more snaps of McCandless going into the country club, where he joined three men for breakfast. In anticipation of the need to blend in with the golf crowd, I had dressed casually, a windbreaker hiding my shoulder holster and piece. I was able to have a nice breakfast myself while keeping McCandless in sight. When the foursome left for the links, I went back to the Studebaker and waited for him to return to his car.

A stakeout like that can be long and boring. Thankfully, the group only played nine holes of golf that morning, finishing around noon. I got more pics of McCandless getting into his car. The last set of pictures was of him entering his house at 12:33. The first part of the job was complete. Next, I would have to get my film developed and make a report to Miller.

**

The security guard at the *Chronicle* called the newsroom to clear me for entry. "Mr. Winston, this is Sam at the front desk. There's a Jake Malloy here to see you. … Okay, I'll send him up." Sam pointed to the elevator. "Third floor and left down the hall."

Gary Winston was waiting for me at the entrance to the newsroom. "Nice to see you again, Jake," he said, shaking my hand. "Come on in."

I followed Winston past rows of empty desks to his glass-walled office, where the door was engraved "Gary Winston, City Editor." Gary's was one of those remarkable success stories, having risen to his present position after starting as an office supply clerk at the paper in the 1920s.

"Want some coffee?" he asked.

"Yeah, thanks. Just black."

"We just wrapped the evening edition. That's why there's no one here except me to meet with you," he said, pouring me a cup of coffee.

"Thanks," I replied, sipping the strongest coffee I've ever had since leaving the coast guard.

"So, tell me your story again."

"Well, it goes like this," I said. "I got two guys, army buddies, murdered this week. I think their deaths are linked to an incident during the Battle of the Bulge. The two of them were together and survived a Nazi massacre of POWs near the Belgian town of Malmedy. The first guy killed, Chuck Darcy, a San Francisco guy, left a blood-stained note we think said Malmedy. They saw the Nazi officer go around and execute any survivors of the machine-gunning. Chuck told his wife he thought he recognized the officer, maybe a client during the time Chuck was a limo driver. The name could be Young or Younger. I've determined Chuck had been doing some of his driving for the German consulate. So, I need to learn more about the consulate."

"That's some story! I think I can help you. I was still on the street beat before the war. I covered all the consulate stories. Got this desk jockey job a couple years back, luckily, before my knees gave in."

"Thanks, Gary. Sorry about your knees."

"Before I let you look at my files, let me give you some background. I think I remember; you're not a native of Frisco."

"That's right. Came here during the war. Liked the city and stayed."

"Well, before the war, there was a lot of pro-Germany sentiment here in the bay area.

We even had a local office of the pro-Nazi group, the German American Bund. I know the FBI was keeping tabs on their activities. The pro-Nazi fervor subsided some after Hitler invaded Poland in September '39. Within a few days after Pearl Harbor, everyone associated with the consulate and Bund office beat it out of the country, but not before burning all their records."

"So, it might be possible that somebody Chuck chauffeured was the Nazi executor at Malmedy," I said.

"Yep, might be. Okay, grab your coffee and follow me."

Gary led me to a small conference room where the table was covered with boxes. "Here are the files with all my stories on the consulate and the Bund. If the Chronicle had a story on them, I wrote it. Have fun. Let me know if you need anything. There's more coffee."

"Thanks, Gary. No more coffee for me. I'm going to dig right in."

Gary had dated the boxes by year. Chuck got his driving job in the fall of 1938 and quit after the Nazi flag incident. I started with the box labeled 1938, worked forward, read every article, and used my camera to copy the texts and any accompanying photos, all the while looking for someone named Young or Younger. I found an article covering the story of the mayor hosting the German consulate and allowing the swastika to stand next to Old Glory.

Halfway through the 1939 box, I found an article headlined, "New York Bund Leader Visits German Consulate." Concentrating on reading the text and the caption, I almost missed looking at the photo. Giving the picture a casual glance on its way back to the folder, I was startled by a possible recognition. The Bund leader, Karl Jung, shaking hands with the German Consul General, looked a lot like my client, Carl Young! I immediately went to talk with Gary.

"Gary, I think I got something. Do you have a magnifying glass?"

"Yeah, sure," said Gary, opening a desk drawer. "Here."

Gary waited patiently while I big-eyed

the photo. Using a magnifying glass on a newspaper photo is tricky. If you try to get too much magnification, the image gets grainy. After optimizing what I could see, I was convinced that Karl Jung was my Carl Young. I put the clipped article on Gary's desk and pointed at the picture. "I think that guy, Karl Jung, is a client of mine, Carl, with a C, Young."

Gary took a look at the photo. "If that's true, that would be some story. I'm going to put one of my hotshot reporters on it."

"Great! That might help me with my investigation." I returned to the conference room and continued going through the files until I got to the one on the Nazi flag incident, then stopped.

Gary was banging the keys of his typewriter when I went to say goodbye. "What are you working on, Gary?"

He laughed. "I'm writing a novel about a cub reporter," tapping his chest, "at a big metropolitan newspaper."

"Interesting concept," I said with a smile. "I'm all done. Didn't find anything else. You ready for those beers I owe you?"

"Nah. I'll take a rain check. I want to keep writing."

"Okay. Thanks for the help. See you later."

"See you later."

***

On my way back to the office, I dropped off my roll of film for developing. The drugstore clerk informed me there were no deliveries on Sunday. I'd have to wait until Monday morning.

I tried unsuccessfully to contact Farrell about Young. That would wait for Monday as well.

CHAPTER EIGHTEEN

I had tried several times, unsuccessfully, to reach Farrell on Sunday. Monday morning, I called at eight. All I got was that Farrell wasn't in; he was out working a case. The best I could do was leave another message.

More frustration, the film delivery truck was late that day. I had to cool my heels at the Hot Stone Bakery across the street. Had some coffee and, yeah, a donut, sitting at a table where I could spot the film guy arrive. When the truck finally got there, forty-five minutes late, I picked up my film and returned to the office. There was barely enough time for me to make it to my ten o'clock appointment with Miller.

Back at my office, I sorted out the pictures

of McCandless's Saturday morning adventures from those of Winston's newspaper clippings. The McCandless photos went into the envelope with the report I had typed up Sunday night.

Before I left, I gave Farrell's office another call. No luck.

***

Miller was a partner at a law firm with an office on Market Street. I arrived a few minutes before my scheduled appointment.

"Jake Malloy, I have a 10:00 appointment with Mr. Miller," I informed the receptionist.

"Yes, Mr. Malloy. Please have a seat. Mr. Miller is with a client now."

In a short time, Miller stepped out of his office, accompanying a ritzy looking dame. He said goodbye to her, then greeted me. "Hello, Malloy. Come in." After we were both seated, he got right down to business. "Guilty or not guilty?"

"Not guilty," I replied.

"I'm pleased to hear that. The McCandlesses are old friends. I wouldn't want to see them having problems."

"I have lots of pictures of him leaving his house, arriving at the Golden Gate golf course, breakfast with three friends, and the foursome starting out on the first hole. I followed him back home after the golfing, got a picture of him entering his house. I've labeled all the pictures with time and place. They're in here with my written report." I placed the envelope on Miller's desk.

"Great. I know you do good work. I will look at this later. I've another client coming in soon," Miller said, standing up. "I assume your bill is in the envelope?"

"Yes, sir."

"Well, then. Good morning, Malloy."

"Good morning," I replied, standing up. "Would it be possible for me to make a phone call before I leave?"

Miller leaned over and pressed a button on his intercom. "Janet, please let Mr. Malloy use the phone in the conference room."

"Thank you, sir. Goodbye."

"Goodbye," replied Miller.

***

The receptionist was on her feet when I exited Miller's office and escorted me to the conference room. She placed a phone on the table. "Here you are, Mr. Malloy."

I called Farrell's office with the dread of another failure. He picked up.

"Mike, I got a suspect in the Darcy/Barbinski murders. It looks like the Nazi from the Malmedy massacre was someone Darcy recognized from his days chauffeuring for the German Consulate before the war. He's back in the States now."

"That's some story! Who's the suspect?"

"He called himself Karl Jung before the war. Now he's Carl Young, with a C instead of a K. Believe it or not, I did some work for him."

"Carl Young? And where does this Carl Young live?" Farrell asked.

"Carolina Street in Potrero Hill."

"Well, my friend, you got yourself a dead suspect. Young was strangled to death sometime yesterday evening. I caught the case."

"That's terrible. I can't believe it!" I said. "What happened?"

"The night butler found him dead, still at his desk, a little after ten. Hanging from Young's neck was a cardboard sign that read NAZI."

"Looks like somebody knew about his past," I offered.

"Yeah, I guess that's the angle."

"What's your theory of the crime, Mike?"

"Here's the way I see it. The killer entered the study through the unlocked door to the patio and came up behind Young. Marks on Young's neck indicate some kind of garrote."

"Any signs of a struggle?" I asked.

"How much struggle could you expect from a paraplegic being strangled from behind?"

"What! Young was a paraplegic?"

"Yeah. You worked for him, and you didn't know?"

"I only met him a few times in his house. He was always seated."

"And you didn't notice his wheelchair?" Farrell asked.

"He wasn't in a wheelchair when I saw

him."

"Sounds like he didn't like being seen that way. His daughter said he was wounded during the war. She doesn't know much of his past. Her parents were divorced when she was two. She grew up living with her mother in Milwaukee, never saw her father. When her mother died, Lisa—that's her name—came to live with her father. I get the feeling things were strained between them."

"Yeah, they argued over her boyfriend, a guy named Bill Hunter. Young had me pay Hunter off with a $10,000 check last week."

"Should I make the boyfriend a suspect?" Farrell asked.

"I don't know how he would know Young's Nazi past."

"I'll at least see if he has an alibi for the time frame. The butler brought Young a glass of wine just before nine, then, like I said, found him dead a little after ten."

I gave Hunter's name and address to Farrell and asked him to let me know of any developments in the case. Then I called Winston at his *Chronicle* office.

"Gary, I just learned that Young was strangled to death last night. The killer left a sign around his neck saying, Nazi. Did you tell anyone about our findings on Saturday?"

"No, Jake, didn't say a word to anyone. I was planning on assigning the story to someone this morning. It sounds like an even bigger story now. I'll get my man on it right away."

I thanked the receptionist for the use of the phone and left for my office.

***

Driving back to the office, I mulled over how or if Young's murder fit into my investigation of Chuck and Lucek's deaths. Young's paralysis ruled him out as their killer, but he had the dough to hire it out. All three victims seemed linked to Malmedy, but that didn't mean their murders were connected. Someone seemed familiar with Young's Nazi past; could be the motive there. Chuck's dying note indicated that his death, and maybe Lucek's as well, was linked to Malmedy. Confused, I found myself at another dead end.

It wasn't yet noon when I parked my car down the street from my office. The time of day didn't deter me. I needed a drink and some company. I went straight to Kelly's.

CHAPTER NINETEEN

Kelly's was empty, except for half a dozen old-timers sitting around a table in a corner. Kelly greeted me. "Jake! What brings you in so early?"

"Ah, got some things on my mind. Let me have a Guinness." While Kelly poured my beer, I asked, "Who are they?" pointing with my head.

"They call themselves the Blarney Stoners. Every one of them born in Ireland. They gather Monday mornings for coffee and Irish soda bread and tell their stories of Ireland. The original group had eight members. They've lost three. The one with the red hair joined recently."

"That's nice," I replied.

"What's got you down? The investigation?"

"Yeah. I thought I had a suspect. Remember, Meg told me Chuck had mentioned the name Young or Younger. I found a guy named Young right here in Frisco. He had been associated with the consulate. He's someone Chuck could have driven."

"Then you got a lead!"

"I thought so until someone murdered him Sunday night. Now I don't have anything."

"I can understand your frustration."

"Yeah," I replied with a shrug. "I think I'd better have something to eat with my beer. Can I get a corned beef sandwich?"

"Okay. I'll be right back."

Kelly left for the kitchen. I sipped my beer and turned to look at the Blarney Stoners. The redhead, who probably had new stories for the group, was talking, animating with his hands. I couldn't hear too much, just enough to tell he was speaking Gaelic.

"Here's your sandwich, Jake," Kelly put a jar of mustard next to the plate. "and here's some mustard if you want more."

"Thanks, Johnny."

"You know, Jake. I've been thinking, remembering those days when Chuck was driving. Then it came to me. Chuck told me one guy he drove gave him a real hard time. Chuck was easy-going, but that guy got to him. Chuck called him 'that bastard Jager.'"

"Jager! Chuck said his name was Jager?"

"Yes."

I couldn't contain my excitement. I pushed my sandwich away. "I've got to go. Put this on my tab?"

"Yeah, sure, Jake," Kelly replied, confusion in his voice.

I left and walked as fast as I could my mind racing.

Back at the office, I pulled out the crime scene photos and found the one with Malmedy written on the tracing paper. I filled in the second word: Jager!

I guessed at what went down that night. For whatever reason, Jager, the Nazi officer from Malmedy, showed up in Chuck's diner. Chuck recognized him, may have called him out by name. "Jager!" Chuck threw the dishes at Jager. Jager pulled out his gun. Chuck went for his gun under the counter. Jager won the draw and shot Chuck, emptied the cash drawer, flipped the open/closed sign to CLOSED, and beat it.

I started a search through Winston's articles all over again. Read all the text and the captions on each picture, looking for the name Jager. I found him! Wilhelm Jager, an official with the Chicago chapter of the German American Bund, addressed a Bund meeting in

San Francisco on August 8, 1939. The photo that accompanied the article showed Jager with the Consul General. I thought I recognized Jager's face and used my magnifying glass for a better look. I had no doubt the Jager in the photo was Bill Hunter, the boyfriend I had paid off with the $10,000 check from Young.

***

Farrell answered the phone after a couple of rings.

"Mike, the second word in Darcy's note is Jager!"

"Jager?" he asked.

"Yes, I believe the note says Malmedy and Jager. The Nazi who did the executions at Malmedy, the Nazi Chuck recognized from his chauffeuring days, was named Jager J-A-G-E-R. Check the picture."

"I got it," responded Farrell. "I agree that's a reasonable interpretation."

"There's more. I found a picture of Jager in the files I got from Winston at the *Chronicle*. Jager, Wilhelm Jager, is Bill Hunter, Lisa Young's former boyfriend."

"Wow! That's some find if it's true. A Nazi war criminal here in the city committing murders. I'll put out an APB on Hunter right away. I'll call the Feds. I'm sure they will be interested in a former Nazi living in San Francisco. You have to step back now, Jake. This is police business."

"Will do, Mike. I hope you catch him soon. Can you let me know what happens?"

"Sure."

***

A shot of Jameson's helped me calm down after the phone call with Farrell. In all my excitement, I failed to notice I had a message on my answering machine. The message was from a lawyer named Harcourt. He had a divorce case in the courts in Reno and needed me to certify the photos I had taken during my surveillance, following a wife to her afternoon trysts. A paid overnight trip to Reno was just what I needed then, and it would help me stay out of the way as I had promised Farrell.

Divorces were typically easy in Nevada, while almost impossible in California.

Californians could go to Nevada and establish themselves as Nevada citizens with a six weeks' stay. Reno, with its casinos and glitz, was a popular place. After a quick divorce, back to California they went. Things were more complicated if there was a fight over assets or custody of the kids. Harcourt's case must have been one of those.

***

Reno was a five-hour drive from Frisco. My old Studebaker struggled climbing the roads into the Sierra mountains. I had called ahead and got a room at the Golden Arm Casino. One of my P.I. school classmates, Kenny (Moose) Musburger, was the house dick there. Nevada and California had a reciprocal agreement on carrying concealed weapons, and Moose always cleared me to carry in the casino. The way things had been going back in the city, I kept strapping on my ankle holster as backup to my shoulder piece. I had a nice dinner with Moose on the house. I arm-wrestled some with the one-armed bandits. Tired from the drive, I hit the sack early.

CHAPTER TWENTY

The casino had a fantastic breakfast buffet, and I lingered until it was time to leave for the hearing. I knew I couldn't take my weapons into the courthouse and left them with Moose. He had worked out a free stay for the second night, so I didn't have to worry over checkout time, unsure of the court schedule. Harcourt had told me to arrive at the courthouse before nine-thirty, and that's all I knew.

Right out of the starting gate, the schedule tanked. Harcourt's case had been rescheduled for two. Didn't bother me; I was getting paid for my time. It was a nice day, so I toured the casino district and made sure to walk under the Reno Arch proclaiming Reno "THE BIGGEST LITTLE CITY IN THE WORLD." Strolling through several casinos, I took time to watch the gamblers. The blackjack players were the most interesting, their facial expressions changing with every turn of the cards. I stuffed myself at a lunch buffet in the Five Diamonds Casino.

Harcourt's case started at 2:10. I was called early and gave my testimony certifying the photos. That was it. Harcourt told me I was free to leave Reno. Returning to the Golden Arm Casino, I got my things, strapped on my shoulder and ankle guns, and said goodbye to Moose.

***

It was dusk when I got back to the city. I had no plans for the evening. After gorging myself twice at the buffets in Reno, I didn't think I'd wanted to eat again for two days. The first thing I needed to do was drop my bag at the office, then maybe go to Kelly's for a drink.

When I unlocked and opened my office door, my key in my right hand, my suitcase in my left, I found myself in a trap. A shadowy figure sitting at my desk simultaneously switched on the desk lamp and ordered, "Stop right there. Hands up." It was Jager, pointing a .38 at me. "Take off your coat, then with just your thumb and forefinger, remove your gun slowly from the holster and toss it in the corner. No tricks." I complied. "Have a seat," he said, pointing with his chin to the stuffed chair.

"Bill Hunter," I announced. "Or should I call you Wilhelm Jager?"

"You are a very clever man, Malloy. You've been a thorn in my side all this time. Now you got the Feds after me."

"I'm sorry to have interfered with your plans."

"That's going to end tonight. I'm leaving the country, first to Mexico. Then I will be joining some Reich brothers in Argentina. I got $10,000 to travel on now. Thought I should stop and say goodbye, settle things with you first."

"I can see that's something you might want to do. Can I ask you a few questions?"

"Yeah, why not? You won't be telling any tales."

"I know you shot Darcy. How did you end up in his diner?"

"I was looking for you," replied Jager. "I was going to buy you off so you wouldn't squeal on Lisa and me to her father. You weren't in your office, so I went into the diner to inquire. That's when Darcy recognized me. I had to shoot him."

"And Barbinski? Was that you?"

Jager nodded. "Yeah. I went to the funeral as a precaution. When I heard Barbinski's eulogy, I couldn't take the chance that he could ID me. I knew he would be at that Irish restaurant and waited for him to leave."

The whole time I was talking with Jager, I was thinking of my ankle piece. I had practiced drawing it dozens of times sitting in that stuffed chair. When Jager ordered me to sit, I placed my hands on my thighs, which is a natural move. I kept my hands there, ready to reach for the .32. All I needed was a distraction. I had to keep him talking while I thought.

"And Young?" I asked.

"Him, too. It just wasn't in the order I had planned, which was to marry Lisa then kill the old man, maybe Lisa, after that. It was all about getting the old man's money. When you gave me that check, I knew I'd never get to marry Lisa while he was alive. So I had to kill him. I had made copies of Lisa's house keys, which made it easy to get into his house."

"And you left the door unlocked as if it was that way all along."

"That's right, Malloy. You're almost as smart as me."

"Didn't you think I would point to you as a suspect?"

"I did—didn't worry me. No weapon, no fingerprints. The cops wouldn't have been able to pin it on me. And I'd be there to comfort Lisa."

I was running out of questions and time. How much longer would Jager play along? He seemed to relish letting me know how clever he was. There was an ashtray sitting on the table next to my chair. I could throw it at him. Even if he fired back, he might be unbalanced enough to miss, and I would have my chance. I had to keep the questions coming.

"How were you, a Nazi, able to immigrate

to the United States?"

Jager laughed. "You Americans are so stupid. All I did was mingle with the war refugees. I applied for entry to the country like thousands of others. Of course, I didn't have any papers. I told them my name was Erick Muller, but I wanted an Anglo name. What a joke. I anglicized my real name, Wilhelm Jager, to Bill Hunter, but you know that already."

"How did you decide to come to Frisco?" I asked.

"Enough questions," Jager barked back at me. "I think it's time to put an end to this."

As Jager was pronouncing my death sentence, a flashing red light penetrated the dimly lit office. Jager turned his head towards the window behind him. "Cops!" he said excitedly.

I drew my .32 and fired.

CHAPTER TWENTY-ONE

Jager and I had fired almost simultaneously. Crouched over to reach my ankle holster, I made a smaller target. Jager's shot got me in the left arm, a flesh wound. My shot, even though rushed, aimed true, hitting Jager in the chest. For a moment, Jager remained upright in his chair, a pained look on his face before his upper body slumped onto the desk. With my right hand still holding my .32, I pressed against my wound and walked to the desk. I used my left hand to remove Jager's .38 from his grip, a precaution that would prove unnecessary.

Seconds later, the door flung open. In stepped Farrell, gun in hand. He gave a quick look around the room. "Jake, are you all right?

What happened?"

"Yeah, just a flesh wound, but it hurts like hell. That's Jager."

Farrell checked Jager for a pulse. "He's dead."

"I guess that's the end of it then," I said. "He confessed to all three murders: Darcy, Barbinski, and Young." I let myself fall into the stuffed chair and placed the two guns on the side table.

"He confessed?"

"Well, more like bragging. He came here to knock me off. I got him talking. He seemed pleased to let me know how clever he had been."

"This is his .38?" asked Farrell, pointing to Jager's gun.

"Yeah."

"I'll have ballistics check it against the bullet that killed Darcy."

"I'm betting it will match," I said. My adrenaline was fading. "Hey, what the hell are you doing here anyway?"

"I'm here with Mrs. Darcy. She begged

me to let her into the diner to get some papers she needed. I told her if she wanted to get in today, I could only do it after work, and it might be late. She didn't care how late; she just wanted to get her papers."

"That explains it," I said, shaking my head.

"Explains what?"

"Explains why Chuck's sign came on, flashing the red light into my office like always. Jager flinched at the flashing red lights, thought it was the cops. See, he had never seen the sign lighted. It was still daylight when he shot Chuck. Chuck hadn't turned the sign on yet. Lucky for me. Jager got distracted just enough for me to get to my ankle holster."

"Yeah, lucky," replied Farrell. "I'm going to call an ambulance for you."

"I guess that's a good idea."

Farrell made two calls: one for the ambulance and one to his precinct to get the medical examiner.

"Look, Jake. I'll let you go now, but I will need to get a full statement later."

"I understand."

"I'm going to go downstairs and wait for the ambulance. I bet Mrs. Darcy is frightened, not knowing what the shots were all about. Are you going to be okay?"

"Sure."

Farrell left, and I sat there staring at a corpse in an on-and-off red glow. A short time later, Farrell was back at the office door with Meg. I heard him ask her, "Are you sure you want to do this?"

Meg didn't speak, just nodded her head yes.

Farrell, holding Meg's arm, escorted her to the front of the desk. She stood there silently, except for muffled weeping, staring at her husband's killer. After a few moments, Farrell ushered her out the door. She didn't say anything to me, just patted my right shoulder on the way out.

The ambulance arrived before the M.E. and took me to St. Francis Memorial. I got my wound dressed and some painkillers, then they released me. I had to check into a hotel. My office was a crime scene.

CHAPTER TWENTY-TWO

Ballistics matched Jager's gun to the bullet that killed Chuck, but Farrell couldn't link Jager to the murders of Lucek or Young. All he had was my statement relaying Jager's admission to the killings. Farrell declared the three cases closed.

When Farrell called in the FBI to hunt for Jager as a former Nazi and a suspect in Young's killing, the truth about Young came out. Winston's hotshot reporter got the scoop and a frontpage byline story in the *Chronicle*. Jung had been an FBI agent assigned to infiltrate the Bund. When the war started, he joined the Counterintelligence Corps of the U.S. Army. After he was wounded and paralyzed on a mission in Europe, he was given his new identity and retired to San Francisco. Young was given a military funeral with full honors and buried at the Presidio National Cemetery. Lisa inherited everything and moved back to Milwaukee.

The new owner renamed the diner, Let's Eat. I stayed in my office until my lease ran out. The *Chronicle* story on Young had given me credit for solving the cases and discovering a former Nazi "with sinister intent." My business picked up nicely after that. I got a new office and a studio apartment, no more living in the office.

Meg moved to Grass Valley and lived with her mother for a while. She opened a small cafe on Mill Street, serving breakfast and lunch. Later, she bought a cottage in the hills with a view of the valley. Whenever my job takes me to Reno, I stop in Grass Valley for a visit.

The End

Frank Kozusko is retired after a full career as a nuclear engineer and submarine officer in the United States Navy and 20 years as a Professor of Mathematics. THIRD BEAT: Writer. Since retiring, he has published stories, in many genres, in online magazines, anthologies, and literary journals. He has self-published three poetry collections, including *"Boomer Bounce: Poems on a Generation,"* and written/illustrated one children's book: *"Can Penguins Fly*?"

Readers voted his story "Links" as the best

in "Paradox: The Inner Circle Writers' Group Crime/Mystery/Thriller Anthology 2019." He is listed in "Who's Who of Emerging Writers 2021."

His recently created 1950's San Francisco Private Eye, Jake Malloy, has appeared online in "Shotgun Honey" and anthologized in "The Trench Coat Chronicles." and "WhoDunit." Jake now has his own novella: "The Bloody Note Murder."

www.frankkozusko.com